"I'll Cut To The Chase,"

Strong said.

"Please do," Katherine answered.

"Somehow, some way, someone never properly filed our annulment papers."

"The bottom line—?"

"I'm not your *ex*-husband, Kit."

"You're not?" she whispered hoarsely.

"As a matter of fact, I'm not your *ex*-anything," he said.

"What are you, then?" she asked.

"Your husband," Strong replied.

"And what does that make me?"

"My wife." He paused. "We're still legally married."

Dear Reader,

I hope you're having a happy winter season, and that you're all reading lots of Silhouette Desire books. This month we have an especially wonderful lineup of love stories, guaranteed to take the chill out of the frosty winter air. (For those of you who live in warmer climates, well, you'll just have to get *warmer!*)

Let's start with Jennifer Greene's *Man of the Month, It Had To Be You.* I know many of you like Ms. Greene's work, because you write and tell me so. And I'm sure you'll find this romance—with its very special hero—making its way to your "keeper" shelf.

Next, there's the third book in Lass Small's delightful series about the FABULOUS BROWN BROTHERS. It's called *Beware of Widows* and I know you'll love this story, written in Lass's unique style.

I'm sure you all remember Suzanne Simms's sparkling, sexy "June Groom" title, *Not His Wedding!* Well, now we have *Not Her Wedding!* Don't worry if you haven't read the first book in this duo; *Not Her Wedding!* stands on its own.

December is completed by some great stuff from ever emotional, ever impressive Karen Keast, *The Silence of Angels;* a new offering from one of my favorites, BJ James, *The Man with the Midnight Eyes,* and some fun from Elizabeth Bevarly, *Jake's Christmas*.

Don't miss a single one of these titles! And until next month, Happy Reading.

All the best,
Lucia Macro
Senior Editor

SUZANNE SIMMS
NOT *HER* WEDDING!

SILHOUETTE *Desire*
Published by Silhouette Books New York
America's Publisher of Contemporary Romance

SILHOUETTE BOOKS
300 East 42nd St., New York, N.Y. 10017

NOT *HER* WEDDING!

Copyright © 1992 by Suzanne Simmons Guntrum

ISBN: 0-373-05754-7

First Silhouette Books printing December 1992

Printed in the U.S.A.

SUZANNE SIMMS

had her first romance novel published thirteen years ago and is "thrilled" to be back at Silhouette Desire. Suzanne has traveled extensively, including a memorable trip to the Philippines, which, she says, "changed my life." She also writes historical romance as Suzanne Simmons.

The author currently lives with her husband, her son and her cat, Merlin, in Fort Wayne, Indiana. *Not Her Wedding!* is her twenty-fifth book.

For two very special friends:
Maureen Walters and Susan James

Prologue

Gold.

It was better than sex.

Gold.

It was better than a hot woman on a bitter cold night.

Gold.

It was better than a shot of his favorite whiskey. It was better than a steak cooked rare and eggs over easy for breakfast. It was better than booze, better than broads, better than a soft bed, better than any bed.

It was a fever. It was an addiction. The gold bug. Once a man was bitten, there was no cure. He took it with him to the grave.

He wanted the gold. He wanted to see it, touch it,

possess it, know that it was his just for a few minutes. Then he could die happy.

He was sorry the past had to be dredged up. Still, he would do whatever was necessary for the gold.

He didn't mean Strong and the girl any harm. But the way he figured it, Michael O'Kelly owed him. Michael O'Kelly owed a lot of people in this town. Too bad the Irishman had died before he'd talked; the bastard could have saved everybody a passel of trouble in the long run.

All he wanted now was the gold.

One

Weddings *were* a waste of time!

Her brother had been right all along. Or perhaps she had simply attended one too many in the past ten years.

Katherine St. Clair tossed the engraved vellum invitation down on her desk, pushed her leather chair back and rose to her feet. She strolled across her office and stood for a moment gazing out the thirtieth-floor window at the lights of downtown Phoenix, Paradise Valley and Scottsdale to the north, Tempe to the east and a good part of the Salt River Valley in between, then looked toward the dark looming shadows of the Superstition Mountains in the distance.

*What was this for Muffy? Husband number three?
Or husband number four?*

Katherine had lost count. Leave it to Muffy Wainwright to throw a gala for each and every wedding, instead of the discreet, private affair it should have been for a third or fourth trip down the aisle.

Muffy always did love a parade.

Katherine leaned over and pressed the button on her dictating machine for the umpteenth time that evening. "Please R.S.V.P. my regrets for the wedding of Muffy—" she gave a tired laugh and corrected herself "—for the wedding of Eleanor Wainwright. And send the obligatory piece of silver with my card. Thanks, Sally. That should take care of the mail."

She flipped off the machine, gathered up the stack of personal letters her assistant had set to one side, stuffed them into her briefcase—she'd read them over a glass of wine once she was home—and walked out the door.

As she turned to lock the office behind her, Katherine studied the discreet lettering on the wall with pride: St. Clair Enterprises.

Most people assumed her father was the major force behind the business.

Most people were wrong.

She had done it with her own talent, her own money and her own determination to succeed—with a little help from the St. Clair family name and connections.

Photographing the rich and famous of the Valley, their luxurious homes and their life-styles paid the bills. The series of black-and-white nature prints she'd done for a book on Arizona and her first one-woman show held in a Scottsdale gallery last year satisfied the soul. She might not be Ansel Adams, but her photographs were fetching surprisingly high prices.

Ridiculously high prices, she sometimes thought.

Then she recalled a human interest article she had recently read in the *Arizona Republic* about a woman who was selling paw prints "painted" by her cat. The watercolors were bringing several hundred dollars and more.

Perhaps her photographs weren't so ridiculously high priced at that, thought Katherine with a rare touch of humor.

She decided to make a brief stop in the ladies' room before ringing for the elevator. She was in the process of pulling up her panty hose when she heard the door of the rest room open and two young secretaries enter. They seemed unaware that any of the stalls were occupied.

"Did you see the outfit *she's* wearing today?" gossiped the first girl.

The second girl sighed with envy. "Yes. It's absolutely gorgeous."

"It should be. I saw the identical designer suit advertised at Lord & Taylor's. The price tag was more than either of us makes in a month."

"That much?" came the stunned reply.

"That much."

"Before taxes?"

"Before taxes."

Sometime during the exchange Katherine's ears began to burn. She had the oddest feeling they were talking about her.

The more sympathetic of the two tentatively issued a compliment, "She *is* beautiful."

"And haughty," the first young woman was quick to point out. "Her nose is stuck up so high in the air, it's a wonder icicles don't form on the end."

After a moment it was thoughtfully suggested, "Maybe she's just shy."

That brought a hoot of laughter from the other secretary and left Katherine squirming behind the stall door. "Shy? The Princess? I don't think so."

"Well, you never know. Look at Princess Di. She's shy and she's real royalty."

With a hint of disdain in her voice, the more cynical girl declared, "Katherine St. Clair was born with a silver spoon in her mouth, and it's been there ever since."

"Well, I wasn't so lucky," said her companion, "so I'd better get back to work before someone comes looking for me. I can't afford to lose my job."

"Neither can I," the other echoed.

"Do you think there will be any more overtime this week?"

The door to the rest room was opened and closed, cutting off the answer to the last question. It was several minutes before Katherine had the nerve to come out from her hiding place.

There was an old adage about eavesdroppers that said they rarely heard good of themselves. Apparently there was still a lot of truth in old adages. As she stood in front of the sink washing her hands, Katherine looked up and caught a glimpse of herself in the mirror.

The Princess?

Is that how other people saw her?

She wasn't blind to what she was, *who* she was. She *had* been born with a silver spoon in her mouth. She *did* dress expensively. She *was* a little cool and aloof, she supposed.

But she knew one thing for certain. Being a princess wasn't all it was cracked up to be. It was hard work. Damn hard work. Not to mention the pressures of privilege. It was a constant vigil to say the right thing, do the right thing, *be* the right thing.

Katherine pushed the button for the elevator and waited for the next one going down. As the gunmetal-gray doors slid apart, the sound of voices raised in heated disagreement could be clearly heard. It had to be several of the attorneys from the floor above her. They were always arguing, or working late. Tonight they were apparently doing both.

"I'm telling you, Tom," a young woman in a conservative navy-blue suit and matching navy-blue pumps was lecturing, "if you try to introduce that kind of circumstantial evidence in court, the judge will throw it out."

The pair of lawyers nodded to her and continued their conversation, but Katherine didn't miss the look that passed between them. She knew only a handful of people in the building by name, but they all seemed to know who she was.

Did everyone call her "The Princess" behind her back, or just the secretarial pool?

As she disembarked from the elevator, one of the regular security guards called out cheerfully from his post in the main lobby. "Good evening, Ms. St. Clair."

"Good evening, Hal."

"You leaving now?"

She switched her imported leather handbag to the other shoulder and replied, "Yes, I am."

"I'll walk you to your car, then." He spoke into the beeper on his shirt pocket for a moment, then made his usual pleasant conversation as they headed toward the parking garage. "Been a lovely spring, hasn't it?"

"Yes," Katherine answered politely.

"Not too hot, not too cold."

"We need rain," she contributed.

The uniformed man laughed. "This is the desert. We always need rain."

Katherine unlocked the driver's side of the sleek dark-green Jaguar and slid behind the wheel. "Thanks for escorting me to my car."

"Anytime, Ms. St. Clair."

"Hal—?"

He paused. "Yes."

Do you call me "The Princess" behind my back, too? she almost blurted out.

Instead Katherine smiled up at him. "Good night, Hal."

He touched the brim of his cap and stepped away from the expensive sports car. "Good night, Ms. St. Clair."

Katherine backed out of her reserved parking space, did a graceful ninety-degree turn and swung onto Central Avenue. As she drove toward her home in Paradise Valley, she could feel the tension slowly ease from her neck and shoulders.

What difference did it make if a couple of the young secretaries in the building had a nickname for her? They were only girls. She was a thirty-two-year-old woman. She'd no doubt been called a lot worse things than The Princess.

Katherine reached up and one by one plucked the hairpins from her chignon, gave her head a good shake and sent the cascade of thick, silky hair down around her shoulders. Her hair was like her older brother Ross's. It appeared brown but quickly bleached to blond in the sun.

And there was plenty of sun in Phoenix and the Valley.

Turning down a narrow side street lined with orchards on either side, she inhaled deeply. Orange blossoms. The desert night was perfumed with their fragrance. She remembered another night when the air had been filled with their scent....

Before the memory could take shape, Katherine St. Clair quickly shoved it into that secret room in her heart and slammed the door shut. Years of practice had taught her what to do. She had become very good at protecting herself from the past.

A familiar litany was repeated again and again in her head.

She wouldn't think about him now.
She would think about him later.
She would think about him later.
She would think about him later....

Later that evening Katherine took a Waterford crystal glass from the cupboard and a bottle of her favorite zinfandel from the refrigerator. She poured herself a glass of wine and took a sip as she slipped out of her Ferragamo pumps. Then she began the task of sorting through her personal mail.

It was the usual batch of chatty letters, thank-you's and pleasant little notes from friends. Near the bottom of the stack was a postcard. It showed a stretch of white beach, a lush green island and an azure sea. It would be from her brother and his bride. They were honeymooning on Maui.

She turned the postcard over and read her sibling's sprawling handwriting. "Having a wonderful time. Wish you were here. Or is it; we're here, wish you were wonderful? Either way, love from Ross and Diana."

Katherine laughed out loud.

She was still chuckling to herself when she came to the last piece of mail.

When she thought about it later she wasn't sure what made her take a second look. But she did.

She carefully scrutinized the standard white business envelope. It was a cheap, common brand sold in dime stores. Her name and the address of St. Clair Enterprises had been typewritten on the front, but the print was lopsided and almost too faint to read. Apparently it had been typed on a machine that needed a new ribbon. There was no return address in the corner or on the back. The postmark was smudged and illegible.

As Katherine stood there with the envelope in one hand and her glass of wine in the other, a strange sense of foreboding washed over her. Her heart began to beat faster; she could actually hear it pounding in her ears. The breath seemed to catch in her lungs, and she couldn't swallow. She had a crazy urge to throw the letter away without even opening it.

But she didn't, of course.

Inserting a table knife under the flap, Katherine slit the envelope along the seam. A single piece of paper, identical in size to the fortune in a Chinese cookie, dropped out onto the kitchen floor. She bent over to retrieve it.

There was a studied frown on her features as Katherine St. Clair raised the slip of paper to the light and read aloud, "The past will come back to haunt you, Mrs. O'Kelly."

She sank down into a kitchen chair, the paper clutched in her hand.

"Mrs. O'Kelly," she repeated in a voice that sounded foreign even to her own ears.

That was all in the past, the distant past. That's where it had to stay. It wasn't supposed to come back and haunt her now. God knows, she'd paid for her mistakes.

Katherine stared down at the paper in her hand.

Strong.

She knew there was no sense in fighting it. It had already begun, that bittersweet journey into the past. She would finally allow herself to think about Strong. Memories of him flooded her mind....

Two

Hot and heavy.

That described the attraction between them. It had been immediate, mutual and decidedly sexual. They had taken one look at each other and had known they would end up in bed together.

It was the summer Katherine turned twenty-two. She had just returned home from a trip abroad. The trip was a graduation present from her parents that had included several weeks in the English countryside and several more touring her favorite haunts in Greece and Portugal.

She was about to start her first job as a photographer for a glossy, upscale Valley magazine. Quite a coup for a young woman just out of college, but no surprise to anyone who knew her.

Whatever Kit St. Clair wanted, sooner or later Kit St. Clair got.

Kit was temporarily staying with her mother and father until the swarm of decorators and painters were finished with her new condominium. Wandering into the huge, bright, Spanish-tiled kitchen of her parents' sprawling Paradise Valley home one morning, she helped herself to a glass of freshly squeezed orange juice. She glanced up and saw a gang of young men working industriously in the backyard.

"What in the world are Mom and Dad having done to the lawn?" she asked the housekeeper, Maria.

"Planting cactus," came the answer.

"Cactus?"

"Saguaro."

"It looks like hot work," she observed, sipping her chilled orange juice.

"Anything is hot work when the temperature is one hundred and ten degrees," stated Maria Gonzales.

"Do we have any lemonade?"

The housekeeper nodded. "Of course."

"How many men are working out there?"

Maria shrugged. "Four. Maybe five."

"Then I'll need five glasses, plenty of ice and a pitcher of lemonade." They made up a tray and Kit headed out to the backyard. Going from worker to worker she offered each one a glass. "Would you like a cold drink?"

"Gracias."

"Thank you."

"Thanks."

As she approached the last man, Kit experienced a moment of uncertainty. There was something about him that was intimidating. It was partly his height. He was tall, at least six-three maybe even six-four. It was partly his build. He was broad through the shoulders, muscular and tough as nails. His back and arms flexed with each movement of the shovel as he dug a deep hole in the hard, parched earth.

He had his back to her. He was shirtless and his skin was tanned a deep bronze from working all day under a hot desert sun. His hair was long and straight and black as midnight. He wore a kerchief tied around his brow and knotted at the back; it made him look a little bit like a savage.

A sheen of perspiration covered his skin. There was a rivulet of sweat that started at the base of his skull and ran down the narrow hollow of his spine, disappearing into the waistline of the faded jeans that rode low on his hips.

"Excuse me," began Kit.

The young man turned, and she was momentarily speechless. He was tall, dark and handsome, but his eyes— Dear God, until that instant Katherine St. Clair hadn't known eyes that color truly existed! They were green. Vivid green. Emerald green. Irish green.

His mixed heritage was written all over his powerful face. Somewhere in his background was Native American—maybe Navajo, possibly Hopi—Hispanic and Anglo. She wasn't sure of the rest. All Kit knew for certain was that standing before her was the most beautiful human being she had ever seen.

"Aren't you going to offer me a glass of lemonade?" he finally asked in a deep, sardonic voice that sent chills down her spine.

She gave herself a shake and laughed, slightly embarrassed. "Yes. Of course. Would you like some?"

He nodded, raised the glass of lemonade to his mouth and drank it down in a single gulp. She watched, enthralled by the bobbing of his Adam's apple.

"Thanks," he said with a hint of a smile. Before returning the ice-cold glass to the tray, he pressed it to his forehead, the hard line of his jaw, his neck, then drew it back and forth across the expanse of his chest. "Sure is hot," was all he said by way of explanation.

Kit's lips were suddenly dry. She lightly ran her tongue over them and found herself wondering what this stranger would taste like.

She was shocked by her own thoughts. He knew the impact he had on her, of course. He was used to the effect he had on women. A man couldn't look like this one did and not be aware of it.

"What's your name?" she blurted out.

He looked down at her for half a minute, then answered, "Strong."

"Strong?" Kit nearly laughed out loud. He was certainly *that*.

He loomed over her. "Strongarm, actually."

Even more appropriate. "Strongarm *what*?"

Challenge appeared on his features as he spelled it out for her. "My full name is Strongarm Carlos Michael O'Kelly."

"Strong O'Kelly."

"That's what I go by."

"I can see why," she murmured.

"What's your name? Your first name, that is. I assume you're a St. Clair."

"Katherine, but my friends call me Kit."

"Are you married, Kit St. Clair?"

This time she did laugh out loud. "What a strange question to ask someone you've just met."

He shrugged his broad shoulders. "I need to know."

She put her head back, raised her right hand to shade her eyes from the harsh glare of the Arizona sun and gazed up at him. "Why?"

"Because I don't take out married women."

"Take out?"

Strong nodded his head. "Date." He went on. "Are you familiar with the Mexican restaurant over on Seventy-fourth?"

Kit heard herself admit to him, "Yes."

"Meet me there tonight at ten."

"Meet you there?"

"Ten o'clock sharp." Then he turned his back and resumed digging.

Empty lemonade glasses and tray in hand, Kit ran for the safety of her parents' house.

Was the man crazy? Meet him at ten o'clock tonight at some two-bit restaurant on the other side of town?

She was Katherine St. Clair, only daughter of the wealthy and socially prominent Rachel and Matthew St. Clair of Phoenix and Palm Springs. She didn't go out with strangers, much less strangers she found working in her parents' backyard.

She wasn't a complete fool.

She was a complete fool.

Kit was telling herself that for the hundredth time as she pulled her convertible into the parking lot of the Mexican restaurant on Seventy-fourth Street.

This was conceivably the dumbest thing she'd ever done, but every time she tried to talk herself out of it she visualized Strong O'Kelly's mesmerizing green eyes in that split second after he'd first turned and looked at her.

What had she seen in those incredible eyes? Intelligence? Yes. Surprise? Yes. Recognition? Possibly. Awareness? Definitely. The man was as attracted to her as she was to him. Kit was willing to bet on it.

In fact, it was the reason for her being here right now, she reminded herself.

Kit pulled into an empty parking space and debated whether she should go inside and try to find him, or wait where she was. But before she could decide, the back door opened and Strong appeared.

She'd wondered if it would happen all over again. It did. At the sight of him her heart began to pound, her mouth went dry, her breathing became voluntary, she had to think about inhaling and exhaling every breath of air.

Strong was dressed in a clean pair of faded jeans, a plain white T-shirt and slightly scuffed cowboy boots. There was a thin gold chain around his neck with a small cross hanging from it. His hair was damp and combed back from his face. He was fresh from a shower.

He sauntered toward her in his lean-hipped way, bent over and rested his forearms on the doorframe of the convertible. A smile slowly appeared on his face. "I wondered if you'd really come."

"So did I," she confessed in a breathless voice.

"Hungry?"

"Yes."

"Me, too." He made a motion with his hand. "Scoot over. I'll drive."

"Don't you want to eat here?" She indicated the restaurant in front of them.

"Nope. I work here. We should eat somewhere else. Trust me." And somehow she did.

Strong slid behind the wheel of her car, shifted into reverse and pulled out onto the street. He took short-cuts, alleyways and side streets—he obviously knew Phoenix like the back of his hand—until he pulled up in front of a small food vendor.

"Hey, Miguel," he called out.

"*Strong, buenas noches.*"

"*Tiene Ud. ¿Algo de bueno?*"

The other man laughed and claimed, "All my food is good."

"Then we'll have two of your special enchiladas and a couple of beers."

"*Muy bien.*"

"*Gracias, Miguel.*"

They took their impromptu picnic to the top of a small bluff overlooking the lights of the city. It was a warm summer night and the air was filled with scents: sweet oleander, citrus trees heavily laden with fruit, blooming flowers, dust off the desert floor.

When they were finished eating they sat and talked.

"How many jobs do you have?" Kit asked, curious to find out more about him.

"Three." Strong didn't expound.

"How old are you?"

He hesitated, took a sip of his beer and answered, "Twenty-one. And you?"

She smiled at him. "I'm twenty-two."

"I've always preferred older women," he confided to her as if it were a private joke between them.

"I don't really know anything about you," Kit blurted out as Strong moved closer.

"I don't really know anything about you," he echoed. "Does it matter?"

She watched his handsome face come closer and admitted the truth. "No."

"It doesn't matter to me, either," he murmured in that split second before he drew her into his arms and kissed her.

It was fireworks on the Fourth of July. It was shooting stars and colliding planets. It was explosive. It was physical. It was primitive.

There was an undercurrent of something dark and dangerous about Strong, something wild and exciting and forbidden. They were as different as night and day, yet they couldn't keep their hands off each other.

Hot and heavy words were muttered in her ear. Then Strong rashly confessed, "I want you. God, how I want you."

Kit St. Clair had always prided herself on behaving in an intelligent and rational manner—until that one tiny moment of truth in her car. Her heart swelled. Her blood raced. Her emotions soared.

Strong became everything. She was lost, and he showed her the way. She was hesitant, and he urged her on. She was shy, and he whispered words of encouragement. She could taste him on her lips, smell him on her skin, feel the imprint of his body on hers.

"I've never felt like this before," she confessed.

He gritted through his teeth, "Neither have I."

"We must be crazy."

"We are crazy," he told her. "Crazy about each other."

"What'll we do?"

"Get married."

"Married?"

"Come away with me now. Tonight. We'll drive over the border and find a justice of the peace."

"Strong—"

"I want to make love to you in a real bed, Kit. I want to make love to you on a white sandy beach, in front of a winter's fire, in a meadow of summer wildflowers. I want to make love to you day and night. I want to make love to you forever."

She could feel herself weakening, giving in, losing the last remnant of her reason. "Oh, God, I don't know," she cried out in frustration.

Strong's vivid green eyes caught and held hers. "I'll only ask once. Will you come away with me?"

Kit looked up at him and knew what her answer would be. "Yes."

They drove all night and were married the next morning by a justice of the peace in a small town just over the border. They stopped afterward at a discount store and bought the cheapest wedding rings they could find. It didn't matter to Kit that it wasn't champagne and roses and two-carat diamonds. She was in love.

They sent her parents a telegram, asking for their blessing. Then they drove again, reaching Prescott and the house Strong had inherited from his grandfather the previous year. They honeymooned at the Stone House for seven days and seven nights.

At the end of one blissful week, they returned to Phoenix and knocked on her parents' door. Her mother greeted them with teary kisses. Her father soberly presented Kit with a private detective's report.

That was the beginning of the end.

Kit hadn't married a man, it seemed, but a boy. Strong had lied to her. He wasn't twenty-one. He was seventeen. . . .

"'Marry in haste, repent at leisure.'" Katherine St. Clair reached up and brushed the back of her hand across her cheek. It came away damp with tears.

She had been Mrs. Strongarm Carlos Michael O'Kelly for one brief week. The annulment took longer, much longer.

It had taken even longer still for her heart to heal. She'd put her trust in Strong and he'd betrayed her. She had never forgiven him for that.

Katherine stood on shaky legs, walked over to the kitchen counter and poured herself a medicinal glass of wine. She drank it down.

She'd learned her lesson about men, about *boys,* the hard way. The price had been high and she had paid dearly for it.

Her relationship with Strong O'Kelly was history. It was dead and buried.

Katherine stared down at the piece of paper still clutched in her hand. The message was permanently burned into her brain. "The past will come back to haunt you, Mrs. O'Kelly."

Why would anyone want to dig up the dead now?

Three

"Hell, yes, I'll want to cross-examine your witness on the stand." Strong O'Kelly laughed into the receiver. "I know. I know. You'd do the same for me. See you in court, Counselor."

He hung up the telephone, sat back in his office chair and stared out the row of original ceiling-to-floor windows that overlooked the main street of downtown Prescott and the courthouse square.

Prescott was his kind of town. Twice, in the 1860s and the 1870s, Prescott had been the capital of the Territory of Arizona. It was tucked into a high mountain valley, along the banks of Granite Creek, and was surrounded by national forest.

The small city in central Arizona was a contradiction in terms. Quaint *and* up-and-coming, old-fashioned *and* modern, set in its ways *and* eager for innovation and new ideas. It was steeped in the history of the gold rush, the stagecoach, the miner and the cowboy. Yet it attracted fresh blood, young blood, from Phoenix and the Salt River Valley on a regular basis.

Ten years ago Strong had come north to forget, to put the pain of the past behind him, to start over. He had ended up staying, attending college and going on to law school.

When old Clarence T. Martin—retired judge, attorney-at-law and one honorable sonofagun—had asked him to join his firm with an eye to taking it over someday, Strong had agreed.

He'd never regretted his decision.

Clarence had died last year, but Strong kept his name next to his on the door out of respect. It was the least he could do for the man who had been his mentor and his friend.

A knock interrupted Strong's reverie.

"Yes—"

A gray-haired matron poked her head around the corner of his office door. "I've got that last batch of letters ready for you to sign, if you have a minute."

"Sure thing. Come on in, Mildred."

He'd inherited Mildred Leeper along with the office and the law firm. She had been Clarence T. Martin's secretary and right hand for thirty years. Now she

was his secretary and his right hand. Mildred was in-
dispensable.

Strong took the pen she handed to him and wrote
his signature on each of the perfectly prepared letters
and legal documents. The woman was a perfectionist.
She probably knew more about the law than ten lawyers ever would.

"I'll drop these off at the post office on my way
home," Mildred informed him.

"Thank you."

"Are you working late again tonight?"

"Just for a few minutes."

Apparently Mildred Leeper had heard that story
before. She scowled and shook her head from side to
side. "You're just like Clarence. All work and no play.
At least try and remember to eat some supper." Her
parting words came trailing back over her capable
shoulders, "And don't forget the manila envelope
marked 'personal' that I left on your desk."

Truth to tell, he'd forgotten all about it.

Strong picked up the envelope now, gave it a cur-
sory glance and tossed it back onto a pile of depositions. He'd read whatever it was later.

With office hours officially over, he unfolded his
long legs, stood and stretched, then walked down a
short, connecting hallway to the kitchenette they
shared with the accounting firm next door. He opened
the refrigerator and helped himself to a can of cold
beer. There was a pizza box with two slices left over
from last night.

"Ah, dinner," Strong muttered with a slightly feral grin, and reached for the cold pizza.

Sometime later, feet propped up on the antiquated radiator behind his desk, the empty pizza box on the floor and half the stack of depositions gone through, Strong suddenly remembered the manila envelope.

He rummaged through the papers in front of him and found it. When he thought about it later, he wasn't sure what made him take a second look.

But he did.

He carefully scrutinized the standard nine by twelve manila envelope. It was a common, inexpensive kind sold in dozens of stores. His name and the address of the law office had been typed on the front, but the print was off-center and almost too light to be read. It had obviously been typed on a machine that needed a new ribbon. There was no return address in the corner nor on the back. The postmark was illegible. For some reason it occurred to Strong that it might have been deliberately smudged.

As he sat there with the envelope in one hand and his can of beer in the other, a funny feeling came over him, a reluctance to pursue this any further. He had a crazy urge to throw the damn thing away without even opening it.

But he didn't, of course.

He tore open one end and a single piece of paper fluttered out onto his desk.

Strong picked it up and read aloud, "The past will come back to haunt you, O'Kelly.'

He frowned and crushed the empty beer can in his fist. What in the hell was that supposed to mean?

There was more. He held the manila envelope upside-down and a sheaf of photocopied documents spilled out onto his desk. He picked up the first page and began to read.

At first Strong assumed it was somebody's idea of a bad joke. Then he came to the pertinent section and he knew it was no laughing matter...even without the threat scribbled across the bottom of the last page.

He bit off a short, explicit oath. His feet hit the floor as he bounded out of his chair. He paced back and forth. Stopped. Then began pacing again.

Under the circumstances, there was only one thing he could do, Strong argued with himself. First thing in the morning he'd have to drive south to Phoenix. Whether he liked it or not, he must contact the woman he had once loved, the woman he had once married, a woman he had deliberately lied to, a woman he hadn't seen in nearly ten years.

Kit St. Clair had a right to know. She had to be told. She must be warned.

Strong stared down at the last page of the document. The words were clearly printed in capital letters: *Better Wed Than Dead*!

Like death warmed over, that's how she felt this morning. Katherine St. Clair grimaced and poured herself a cup of coffee. Maybe she'd drink it. Or maybe she'd just pour it over her head.

She hadn't slept well last night. It wasn't just the mysterious note that had kept her awake until the wee hours. It was Strong. Once she'd started thinking about him, she couldn't seem to stop.

She could still envision Strong O'Kelly as he had appeared that first day in her parents' backyard. Tall, dark, heartbreakingly handsome. He had been all rippling muscle and smooth skin bronzed a deep golden brown by the desert sun. She'd never met anyone like him before. He had exuded an animal magnetism, a raw sexuality, that she'd found irresistible.

Then there had been his eyes.

She would never forget his eyes.

Katherine gave herself a good shake. She had extricated Strong O'Kelly from her heart and soul a long time ago... although she confessed to occasionally wondering where he was, what he was doing, *how* he was doing.

"Don't be an idiot, Katherine," she lectured herself as she stood gazing out her office window at bustling downtown Phoenix, the cup of steaming black coffee in her hand. "It's been ten years. It's ancient history. Dead and buried. Don't go looking for trouble. Chances are you'll never see the man again."

The telephone on the desk gave a shrill ring. Then another. She jumped, and picked it up. "Yes."

Her assistant announced over the interoffice line, "There's someone here to see you."

She frowned, and set her cup of coffee down on the desk. "Do they have an appointment?"

"No."

"Who is it?"

"He didn't give his name."

"It's a man?"

"It certainly is."

"What does he want?"

Sally Bradford lowered her voice and spoke directly into the receiver. "He didn't say."

Katherine wasn't in the mood for games this morning. "Didn't or wouldn't?"

Sally hesitated, then confirmed, "Wouldn't."

She sighed and rubbed her left temple where it had begun to throb. Her visitor was undoubtedly one of two things: a salesman or a client. The former was always trying to sell her photographic equipment and supplies. The latter must, of course, he handled with tact and diplomacy. It would never do to alienate a potential client. After all, it was word of mouth that had gotten her where she was today.

Matter-of-factly Katherine inquired, "What color are his shoes?"

"What color are his shoes?" echoed Sally, forgetting to lower her voice.

"Yes, what color are the man's shoes?" she repeated with a kind of weary emphasis. It had been her experience that salesmen had an unfortunate tendency to wear brown footwear.

After a moment her assistant replied, "He's not."

"He's not *what?*"

"Wearing shoes."

Katherine knitted her brows. "What is he wearing, then?"

"Cowboy boots."

She took a minute to digest that bit of information. Sally added unnecessarily, "He's a cowboy."

Katherine couldn't resist the obvious comeback to that announcement, "Yippee."

Sally laughed. After a moment she apologized, "Excuse me, Katherine."

She could hear the deep, sardonic tones of a male voice as the unscheduled visitor said something to her assistant. Sally giggled in response.

Sally Bradford was a Phi Beta Kappa. Sally Bradford never giggled.

"Sally?"

The sophisticated young woman in the outer office came back with an embarrassed laugh. "The gentleman insists that he's actually more Indian than cowboy." She added under her breath, "I can't believe he heard me call him a cowboy."

"Well, I don't care what the gentleman is," Kit muttered, massaging her head. "I don't want to see any cowboys *or* Indians this morning. I don't want to see anyone. Did you tell him I'm busy?"

"I did."

"And?"

"He said he would wait."

Great, he was the persistent type. It was just her luck. "Did you ask the man his business?"

"I tried to. He informed me it was personal. I believe you should see him."

"Why?"

Sally dropped her voice to an intimate level. "Because he's gorgeous."

"Gorgeous?"

"A major hunk."

"Good grief."

"I don't see a wedding ring."

"That doesn't mean he isn't married," she felt compelled to point out.

Sally continued to extol their visitor's virtues. "He's tall. He has black hair and broad shoulders and the most incredible green eyes I've ever seen."

Kit went very still. Suddenly she couldn't seem to breathe. "Green eyes?" She could hear the man speaking again. Her heart began to pick up speed until it was racing in her chest. "Did you say green eyes?"

"Just one moment, please."

"Sally?"

"Katherine—"

"Yes."

"I think you should definitely talk to the man." There was something in Sally Bradford's tone. Something akin to shock.

"Why?"

"Because he claims he's your husband."

Four

***

Husband?

Could it be—?

Dear God, it *was*.

Strong had his back to her when Katherine opened the door of her office, but she knew in an instant it was him. There were some things a woman never forgot about a man: the shape of his ears, the way the hair at his nape brushed the top of his shirt collar, the way he stood, feet planted firmly apart, hands resting on his hips.

She *had* forgotten how tall he was, how broad and muscular through the upper arms and the shoulders. How imposing his sheer physical size could be. He dominated a room simply by walking into it.

"Strong?" It didn't sound like her voice.

He turned and gave a brief nod of his head in acknowledgment. "Kit."

His eyes were just as she remembered them: emerald green in color, bright with intelligence, observant, perceptive, sometimes uncomfortably so. They were also older and wiser, and definitely colder, like two brilliant-cut gemstones.

The straight black hair was shorter, she noticed, less shaggy. The face had matured; the features had hardened. The jawline was chiseled out of Arizona granite. There was no softness to the man, no compromise, no give.

He was dressed in a clean pair of well-washed jeans, a plain white dress shirt and a black leather sport coat. Instead of a traditional tie, there was a silver and turquoise bolo around his neck. An intricate Navajo concha belt encircled his lean waist. There was a Stetson clasped in his hand. She glanced down at his feet. He was wearing hand-tooled leather cowboy boots.

Good Lord, Sally was right. He was a cowboy.

"What are you doing here?" she blurted out.

Lowering his voice to a confidential level, Strong replied, "It might be better if we discussed the matter in private."

Katherine's face burned. "Of course." Somehow—she was never quite sure how—she made the necessary introductions. Indicating the young woman behind the front desk, she said with excruciating politeness, "This is my assistant, Sally Bradford. Sally, my *ex*-husband, Strong O'Kelly."

"Please accept my apologies for being uncooperative earlier, Ms. Bradford," Strong drawled with disarming charm. "I wanted to surprise Kit."

He had certainly managed to do that, thought Katherine wryly. Strong was the last person she'd expected to see in her office this morning.

She turned to Sally. "Would you please hold my telephone calls?"

"Of course, Katherine."

She knew the other woman was bursting with curiosity. To Sally Bradford's credit, it didn't show in either her voice or her manner.

"Shall we go into my office?" she suggested to the man looming over her.

"After you," Strong said with a hint of a sardonic smile and a sweep of his Stetson.

By sheer willpower alone, Kit kept her voice from quavering as she went through the motions of playing the confident business executive, the perfect hostess, The Princess. "I was just having a cup of coffee. Would you care to join me?" she inquired nonchalantly.

"No. Thank you," Strong responded with the same nonchalance.

She gestured toward an upholstered chair in front of her desk. "Won't you sit down?"

"Not yet. Thanks, anyway." Now that he was within the inner sanctum of St. Clair Enterprises, Strong seemed to be in no particular hurry to explain the reason for his visit. He strolled around the expensively decorated office, taking his own good time in examining the colorful kachina in a recessed corner niche, the collection of hardcrafted baskets—Navajo, Piman, Southern Paiute, Pueblo, Hopi, even Apache—arranged on a tabletop, the silver and turquoise Indian jewelry displayed in a lighted cabinet.

"I didn't know you were a collector," he commented offhandedly.

She was tempted to tell him there was a great deal about her that he didn't know, that he had *never* known. Instead Kit bit her tongue and said simply, "I've been collecting for about five years."

He bent over the display case and made a closer study of a Navajo bracelet featuring the twisted-wire technique, a Zuni mosaic brooch of turquoise, jet and clam, spiny oyster and mother-of-pearl, an antique squash-blossom necklace. "I confess I'm no expert, but you have some exceptionally fine pieces here," Strong offered.

"Yes, I do."

He added, "Hard, gem-quality, untreated turquoise is very rare."

"Yes, it is." Katherine took a tentative step in his direction. "My prized possession is the necklace in the center," she said, pointing to the piece. "It was crafted by Slender Maker of Silver."

That statement brought the handsome head up. "*The* Slender Maker of Silver? The one in the famous photograph taken by Ben Wittick?"

"The very one," she said, confirming that its creator had been one of the first and foremost Native American jewelry makers of the past century, a craftsman renowned for his work. "In fact, this particular necklace has been dated to 1885. The same year it's believed the Wittick photograph was taken." Kit went on enthusiastically. "It is the elemental beauty of the early work by Navajo silversmiths that interests the serious collector, of course."

Strong shot her a sideways glance. "My great-grandmother, Rainbow Woman, used to say it was because The People saw beauty as the balance and harmony of all things in nature."

She nodded. "The Navajo concept of *hozho*."

Green eyes glittered. "You know of *hozho*?"

"I know of *hozho*." Unwittingly Kit sighed. "I attempt to find the same balance and harmony in nature with my camera, but it is difficult."

Strong gazed up at the wall of framed photographs. "Yours?" he asked without turning.

"Yes."

He stroked his chin. "I seem to remember you were always lugging a camera around with you."

She couldn't argue with that; it was true. When he'd known her she had always had a camera in her hand. She still did, for that matter.

He finally said, "You're very good."

"Thank you."

He paused in front of a black-and-white enlargement of a favorite photograph she had taken of a storm brewing over the desert. Roiling clouds and bolts of jagged lightning filled the night sky. There was a silhouette of a single saguaro in the foreground, its advanced age evident by the number and size of its thick arms. Behind the cactus was the outline of a towering mountain range.

"I can almost hear the thunder in the distance," Strong murmured under his breath, "and smell the coming rain."

"It was wild and wonderful out in the desert during the storm. Primitive. Powerful. The electricity in the air made my hair stand on end," she related.

His features tightened with disapproval. "You took some risks getting that shot."

"I got soaked to the skin and nearly froze to death, but it was worth it." She'd flirted with danger that night, yet she had never felt so alive.

The same could be said of the one week she had spent as Mrs. Strongarm Carlos Michael O'Kelly.

"Do you have a name for this particular picture?" he asked in an inquisitive tone.

"Yes." How had he guessed? "I call it 'The Gods Are Angry. The Gods Are Pleased.'"

It was impossible to tell whether or not Strong understood.

After a moment he ventured, "Nature reminds us that life is a paradox. We pray for rain and it pours. We pray for sun and it dries up all the rain. What is good for us can also be bad for us." He stepped away, shaking his head. "What we love we often destroy."

He did understand. She should have known he would. Strong had always had a quick mind.

He circled the room, then paused at the window and looked out at the city, the valley, the mountains on the horizon. He grunted. "Nice view. Must cost you a fortune in rent."

"It does." She picked up the coffee cup, but her hands were trembling so badly that she immediately set it down again.

Strong placed the Stetson on a table behind him, then sat down in the upholstered chair. He filled the chair. He filled the room, for that matter. He had always been a little larger than life.

For the first time since entering her private office, he looked directly at her. His expression was unreadable. "How have you been, Kit?" He might have been a stranger inquiring after her health or the weather.

"Fine. And you, how have you been?"

"Fine."

Ten years.

Ten years since they'd parted—she in tears, he in anger—and all they could think to say to each other was. "How are you?" and "I'm fine?"

Ten years.

How she had loved him. How he had loved her. Yet, in the end, they had destroyed that love and each other.

Ten years.

She was no longer a naive and trusting girl, but a woman of thirty-two. Strong was twenty-seven, but he looked older. He acted older, too. He always had. Sometimes Kit wondered if he had ever been a boy like other boys. Now she wondered if he was a man like other men.

Either way, he was still the most beautiful human being she had ever seen.

Katherine swallowed the lump in her throat and reminded herself to keep breathing. "I'm sure you didn't drop in after all this time to tell me what a nice view you think I have from my office."

His mouth twisted. "No, I didn't."

"What is it you want, then?"

"Answers."

"Answers to what?"

"A few questions." He crossed one long muscular leg over the other and studied the design in his boot for a moment before glancing up. "Are you married, Kit?"

She couldn't help herself. She laughed out loud. It was not a laugh of merriment. "You asked me that once before. It got me into a lot of trouble."

Strong persisted. "Are you?"

Kit wet her lips with her tongue and drew in a deep breath. "Am I what?"

"Married. I need to know if you're married," he repeated interrogatively.

She crossed her arms as if she were hugging herself—or holding herself together. "Funny, that's what you claimed the last time, you *needed* to know."

He scowled. "Did I?"

"Yes."

A muscle in his jaw jumped. "Refresh my memory."

She faced him, her lips wearing a lame smile. "It was the first day we met."

The light of recognition dawned in his eyes. "Your parents' backyard."

"You were planting cactus."

"It was hotter than hell."

"Nearly one hundred and ten degrees."

"You brought out a tray of cold drinks."

"Lemonade."

"I remember now," said Strong.

She deliberately put the large mahogany desk between them and sat down. She quirked a brow and inquired in the same interrogative voice he'd used, "Are you married, Strong?"

He answered her question with another question. "Do you know much about the law?"

She shrugged her shoulders. "Some."

He reached into the breast pocket of his leather coat and withdrew a packet of papers. Then he leaned forward and tossed them onto her desk. "Then this will interest you."

Katherine picked the papers up, unfolded them and began to read. It was several minutes before she realized what she was holding. "This appears to be a copy of our annulment."

"It is," he replied coolly, casually stretching his long legs under the desk.

"I'm afraid I don't understand." She made that admission cautiously.

"Someone deliberately sent those papers to me. They arrived at my office yesterday."

"That's odd."

"Yes, it is."

She still didn't have a clue. "I don't get it."

He went on smoothly, his eyes on her all the while. "There is something peculiar about those annulment papers that a good lawyer would spot in five minutes."

Kit spoke to her hands. "Then why mail them to you?"

"I'm a damn good lawyer."

Her head shot up. "I—I'm sorry. I didn't know. I had no idea."

"I didn't expect you to."

Her curiosity was aroused. "When?"

"I passed the bar three years ago."

She continued to digress. "Where do you practice?"

"Prescott."

"Congratulations."

"Thank you." Then Strong added in a hard, dry voice, "It was your doing."

"My doing?"

He sprang to his feet and began to pace back and forth in front of the office window. Then he stopped and speared her with a look that no doubt had left more than one witness trembling in his shoes. "You see, Katherine—" Strong never called her Katherine unless he was very angry with her "—I could never understand how man and his man-made laws could put asunder what God had joined together."

She squirmed in her chair and uttered a quick prayer that this wasn't going to turn ugly. "It was a long time ago, Strong. Let's not dig up the past now."

He laughed darkly. "We may not have any choice. You know what they say, sweetheart..." the last word was anything *but* an endearment.

Kit was loath to ask but she did. "No, I don't know. What do they say?"

He gave her a long, hard look. "The past will come back to haunt you."

She paled. "It was *you?*"

His jaw dropped. "Huh?"

She glared at him accusingly. "It was you who sent that lousy note to me?"

"Lousy note? Hell, no," he swore. "Don't tell me you got one, too?"

"Too?"

"'The past will come back to haunt you, O'Kelly,'" Strong recited from memory.

"Mine said, 'The past will come back to haunt you, Mrs. O'Kelly.'"

Strong ran an agitated hand through his thick, black hair and bit off a harsh, crude expletive. He shot her an unapologetic look. "When did you get yours?"

"Yesterday."

"At home or at the office?"

"Here at the office, but I didn't open it until I got home last night."

"What kind of envelope was it?"

"A plain, inexpensive business-letter size."

"Did you keep it?"

She nodded. "It's at my house."

His eyes narrowed. "How big was the note?"

She considered his question. "It was small, like the paper in a fortune cookie."

"Damn. Damn. Damn."

"What?"

"I got my 'fortune' in a plain manila envelope yesterday, along with that photocopied document." He began pacing again. "Did you read it all the way through?"

She glanced down at the papers in her hand. "No."

"Keep reading."

Kit read. When she came to the last page and saw the threat scribbled across the bottom of the paper, the blood rushed from her head to her feet. Her voice was husky as she said aloud, "'Better wed than dead!' What does it mean?"

"I don't know for sure," he confessed. "Do you understand the legal ramifications of what is contained in the document?"

"I think so. I guess so."

Strong reached across the expanse of mahogany desk and gripped the fingers of her right hand. "Do you or do you not understand?"

Katherine knew the color came up in her face like a red flag. "I don't understand. Perhaps you'd better tell me since you're the lawyer."

"I'll cut to the chase."

"Please do."

"I'll give you the bottom line."

"The rock-bottom line."

"Some how, some way, someone never properly filed our annulment papers."

"They weren't properly filed," she echoed.

He nodded. "It's a technicality. But the law of this land and the state of Arizona is chock full of technicalities."

"The bottom line—?"

"I'm not your *ex*-husband, Kit."

"You're not?" she whispered hoarsely.

"As a matter of fact, I'm not your *ex*-anything." Her voice grew stronger. "What are you, then?"

"Your husband."

Kit was very glad she was already sitting down. "And what does that make me?" She wanted it spelled out.

"You are my wife."

"The annulment?"

"It was never valid."

She whitened. "Meaning?"

"We're still legally married."

Five

She looked like hell.

She was beautiful—perhaps even more beautiful now than she had been at twenty-two—but she still looked like hell. Kit's face was suddenly so pale Strong could see the veins beneath the surface of her skin.

Maybe he should have found another way of telling her. Maybe he shouldn't have sprung it on her like that out of the blue. It wasn't every day, after all, that a woman found out she was still married to her ex-husband.

Strong lifted his black leather shoulders in a shrug. As his dear, old Spanish-speaking *abuela* had been fond of saying, *Qué será será*. Roughly translated into

English, it meant the chips will fall wherever the chips will fall.

So be it.

That was life.

He ran his eyes over the elegant woman on the other side of the desk. "You all right?"

"Am I all right?" she echoed.

"Yes, are you all right?"

Kit shook her head in disbelief. "Married?"

"Yup."

She looked up at him with huge eyes. "Are you sure?"

"I'm sure."

He watched her stare at the document in her hand. "All these years we've been married."

"That's about the size of it."

"I can't believe it."

"Believe it."

"We're husband and wife."

"In the eyes of the law. Now will you answer my original question? Are you married to someone else, Kit?"

Her lips folded in that soft obstinate line he remembered so well. There had been only one way to deal with Kit when she chose to dig in her heels and turn stubborn as a mule. Somehow Strong didn't think this was the time or the place to kiss her until neither of them could think straight.

"Why is it so important?" she insisted.

He summed it up in one word. "Bigamy."

Her hand flew to her mouth. "Ohmigod."

"Are you married?"

"No."

He relaxed a little and took his seat again. "That's a relief, anyway."

She bounced right back with, "Are you?"

"No." He deliberated, his black brows drawn together. "It will make it a whole lot simpler in the long run that neither of us has remarried."

The skin around her mouth was taut. "I don't understand how this could have happened."

"Neither do I."

"My father took care of everything."

He frowned at the mention of her father. Matthew St. Clair was not one of his favorite people. Although, in time, Strong had come to understand the man's love and devotion for his only daughter, his desire to protect her, especially when she was young and beautiful and innocent.

She'd also had a pedigree a mile long: the daughter of money, the granddaughter of money, even the great-granddaughter of money. She had been—she still was, for that matter—the product of generations of good breeding and class.

He, on the other hand, was a mongrel.

He was the son of poor but proud parents, equally poor but proud grandparents and great-grandparents. His was a rich cultural heritage of Native American, Hispanic, Irish and Anglo. But he knew only too well what it is like to be judged on the basis of that mixed heritage.

Strong put it out of his mind and got back to the business at hand. "Who arranged the annulment?"

"A good friend of Dad's. The poor man died of a heart attack last year," she explained.

Strong knew there was the faintest hint of scorn in his tone when he concluded, "He may have been a good friend, but he wasn't a good lawyer."

"We're all human." Kit jumped to the dead man's defense. "We all make mistakes."

"Well, this particular mistake was a real dilly."

"Then we'll just have to take the necessary steps now to correct it," she said icily.

He came straight to the point. "How do you propose we do that?"

She seemed to be choosing her words. "We can quietly get an annulment, or a divorce, or take whatever legal action is required to dissolve our marriage."

He flicked at an imaginary speck of dust on his black leather boot. "You're forgetting one thing."

"What's that?"

"Somebody out there—" he made a vague gesture toward the window and the world beyond "—knows all about this. Somebody, apparently, who isn't interested in us getting an annulment, or a divorce. At least, that's the implication in the threat."

He waited as his ex-wife—hell, she was still his wife—blew out her breath expressively and exclaimed, "Of course!" It finally seemed to dawn on her. " 'Better wed than dead!' "

"Exactly."

"But who?"

"I honestly don't know."

"Could it be a hoax?" she asked in a slightly distorted tone of voice.

Strong shook his head slowly from side to side. "A hoax doesn't make sense. Someone went to a hell of a lot of trouble to get his hands on our annulment papers."

She tried again. "Could it be a practical joke?"

"It could be," he allowed.

Kit's face clouded with concern. "Perhaps someone is trying to embarrass my family."

"That's always a possibility."

"Maybe someone is acting out of spite, or jealousy, or even envy."

He thought about it for half a second. "You're beautiful, talented, and have money to burn, Kit. That does leave a little room for the baser emotions."

She appeared to make up her mind about something. "Muffy."

"Muffy?"

"Muffy Wainwright." She went on to explain. "Her real name is Eleanor. She's had it in for me ever since I got the lead in our senior play and she had to settle for being my understudy. I know it sounds silly, but Muffy has always been one to hold a grudge. I was homecoming queen in high school. She was runner-up. We were both in the choir, but I was asked to sing the solo. I was valedictorian of our class—"

"Don't tell me," he interjected, "Muffy was salutatorian?"

Katherine St. Clair nodded her head and tapped a perfectly manicured nail against her bottom lip. "Coincidentally—or perhaps *not* so coincidentally—an invitation to yet another Wainwright wedding arrived here at the office yesterday."

"I take it Muffy is the blushing bride."

"Not quite the blushing bride. This is the woman's third, maybe even fourth trip down the aisle in less than ten years."

A sardonic smile touched the edges of his mouth. "She's been a busy lady."

The cultured voice was clipped. "Believe me, Muffy Wainwright is no lady."

Strong chuckled.

Kit made a point of informing him, "She has a divorce lawyer on her payroll full time. I'm sure it's a very lucrative business for an attorney."

For some reason he felt obliged to defend himself. "I wouldn't know. I don't handle divorce cases." He cleared his throat. "Any other suspects?"

"My father could have enemies," she suggested reluctantly. "Most successful, powerful, wealthy men make enemies somewhere along the way."

He was following her words with the closest attention. "Why not send the information directly to him, then? Why send it to us?"

She hunched her shoulders. "I don't know."

This wasn't getting them anywhere, in his opinion. Kit leaned forward eagerly. "What about you?"

"What about me?"

"The photocopied papers with the threat scribbled across the bottom were sent to you, not to me. Do you have any enemies?" She dropped the question with complete aplomb.

Strong scowled and thrust out his jaw. "There isn't a lawyer worth his salt who doesn't have some enemies."

"See!"

"No, I don't see."

"It could be some vindictive criminal you've put away. Now he's out of prison and out for revenge."

"I'm not a prosecuting attorney, Kit," he pointed out. "I have a private law practice and deal almost exclusively with civil suits."

Her face fell for a moment. Then she quickly brightened. "A love affair gone bad?"

He shook his head. "Nope."

"A woman scorned?"

He shook his head a second time. "Nope."

"Your secretary is secretly in love with you?"

This time he laughed out loud. "Mildred Leeper is old enough to be my mother." He corrected himself. "Make that my grandmother." He drummed the arm of the chair. "Something tells me we're barking up the wrong tree."

"What makes you say that?"

"Call it a hunch."

She looked at him askance. "A hunch?"

He fought to sound neutral as he said, "It's the masculine version of feminine intuition."

Kit threw up her hands. "Oh, great!"

Her skepticism didn't deter him. He'd gone up against far greater odds again and again in the courtroom. "We have to ask ourselves who has the most to gain. What do they hope to gain?" Their eyes met. "Exactly what is their motive?"

"Yes, Counselor."

"Am I sounding like an attorney?"

"What do you think?"

Strong had the good graces to laugh at himself. "Sorry. I guess it's habit. We do need to consider two things though, Kit. *Why?* And why *now?*"

She sighed, picked up the cup at her elbow, took a sip and grimaced. "I think I'll get myself a fresh cup of coffee. Would you like some?"

He shook his head and muttered under his breath, "I don't understand it. Who would want us to stay married?"

"I can't think of a single person," volunteered Katherine St. Clair as she added a level teaspoon of sugar to her coffee and stirred.

"There's something we haven't figured out yet," he mumbled, rubbing his chin.

"Or something we haven't been told."

He watched as she absentmindedly added more sugar to her coffee and kept stirring. "Go on," he urged.

"None of it makes any sense. It's like a jigsaw puzzle with half of the pieces missing," she said as she walked back to her desk and sat down.

She was right. They didn't have the whole story. Not by a long shot.

"You know, you wouldn't have made a bad attorney, yourself." Strong meant it as a compliment.

Apparently Kit decided to take it as one. "Thank you."

"This could simply be the first skirmish of the battle," he ventured to guess, not really knowing.

"It could be."

"Then again, we may never hear another word about it."

"We may not."

"I might be making more out of this than it deserves." His tone conveyed a shrug.

"You might be."

"I don't want to scare you—"

She raised an elegant eyebrow. "Then don't."

"I assume you have a good security system at home."

"The best."

"Naturally." He straightened the silver and turquoise bolo. "Your office building seems adequately guarded. I had to do some fast talking and show three forms of ID downstairs to get by someone named Hal."

That brought a smile to the beautiful face across from him. "He probably made you check your gun at the door, too."

Strong frowned. "Gun?"

"I was joking," she explained.

"Is Hal a friend of yours?" he asked sharply.

"He occasionally escorts me to my car, especially if I work late." There was a hint of reproach in her voice;

it was directed at him. "Hal is also happily married and the father of three rambunctious little boys."

"I see."

Kit obviously had other things on her mind besides the security guard. "I still think there is a personal vendetta involved."

"Back to your revenge theory?"

"Someone is playing with us, Strong. And I, for one, don't like being played with," she stated, her aristocratic chin held high.

"Neither do I," he concurred.

She looked straight into his eyes, and he suddenly realized it was still there—the sensual awareness, the desire, the need, the electricity that sizzled between them. Strong could feel it right down to his bones.

Damn it all to hell, he thought he had gotten Kit St. Clair out of his system a long time ago.

"What do you think?"

Strong gave himself a shake and had to ask, "About what?"

"Is either of us in any real danger?"

He gave a noncommittal grunt. "Hell, I don't know. I don't think so, but there are plenty of un-happy—and unhinged—people running around loose in the world."

"The police couldn't do a thing to help even if we took them the notes, could they?"

He wasn't going to lie to her. "Frankly, there isn't enough to go on."

She fiddled with the handle of her coffee cup. "The gossips and reporters would have a field day if they got their hands on the story."

"Within twenty-four hours it would be in every newspaper west of the Pecos." He had no doubts about that. The St. Clairs were always news in this part of the world.

Her eyes were stretched wide now and her voice was a mere whisper. "I've worked so hard to build a reputation as a serious businesswoman."

She sounded suddenly quite human, Strong realized. Not like a princess at all.

"It's not exactly the kind of publicity a reputable lawyer desires, either," he agreed grimly.

"What should we do?"

He regarded her for some seconds before he answered. "For now, nothing. Let's just keep it between the two of us."

She was visibly relieved.

He was already having second thoughts. "Take no chances. Watch your back. Call me if anything unusual happens. And I do mean *anything*."

"I will."

That wasn't good enough. Strong pushed her for more. "You have to promise, Kit."

She nodded. "I promise." She swallowed and said a little unsteadily, "I assume that you will see to our mutual legal problem."

"I'll see to it," he growled.

Then there was dead silence in the room.

Strong dug out his wallet and removed a business card. He scribbled on the back and tossed it onto her desk. "This is the motel where I'm staying tonight. The telephone number of my Prescott office is printed on the front. I'll be heading back home first thing in the morning."

She stood and said regally, "Thank you for coming." It was a definite dismissal.

It seemed ridiculous, but he responded, "You're welcome."

She offered her hand. "Take care of yourself."

Strong didn't want to shake her hand. He realized he didn't trust himself to touch her. "You, too."

"Goodbye, Strong."

He slid noiselessly to his feet, blindly thrust out his hand and pumped her arm once. "Adios, sweetheart."

He was out the door of St. Clair Enterprises, in the express elevator and speeding down past the tenth floor before he realized what he had done. The words echoed in his brain like a bitter refrain.

Adios, sweetheart.
Adios, sweetheart.
Adios, sweetheart.

They were the same words he'd flung at Katherine St. Clair when he had walked out of her life ten years ago.

Ten years ago.

Hell, the past had already come back to haunt him.

* * *

Strong was still brooding about the past when he unlocked the door of his motel room after dinner that night. He was feeling pretty morose.

Nothing had changed.

Kit was still caviar and French champagne; he was tortillas and beer.

She was a sleek Jaguar; he was a beat-up four-wheel-drive Jeep.

She was a blue blood, a thoroughbred; he was a mixed breed if there ever was one.

Katherine St. Clair was elegant, sophisticated and cultured. Her hair was like silk. So was her skin. And she smelled so damn good.

He had forgotten how good she smelled.

Stong closed his eyes and inhaled deeply. The faintest hint of her perfume still clung to him.

For a moment he allowed himself to imagine how it would be to take Kit in his arms again, to bury his face in her hair, to undo the buttons of her blouse and push the flimsy lace of her bra aside.

He would skim his hands over her naked flesh, lower his mouth and find her breast waiting for his kiss, his caress. He would gently catch her nipple between his teeth, and nip and tug, tease and lick and suckle until she implored him to take pity on her. Ah, such sweet revenge to hear her cry out for him, to beg him to finish what he had begun.

Then, and only then, would he raise her hips and drive his body into hers again and again until they were both speechless, mindless creatures of pure passion....

"Shit!" He was as hard as a rock.

Strong threw the room key down on the bed in self-disgust, and quickly began to undress.

He padded barefoot to the bathroom, grabbed a towel from the rack next to the shower and flipped on the faucet. He stepped into the cubicle, turned the handle and let the spray of ice-cold water run down his traitorous body.

He wasn't stupid.

He wasn't crazy.

He wasn't a fool.

He certainly wasn't a glutton for punishment.

The woman had turned his guts inside out once before and left him for dead. He wouldn't let it happen again. Not in a million years.

He would never allow Kit, or any woman, to sink her claws into him a second time. He had learned his lesson about women, about females, the hard way.

To hell with all of them!

Six

Kit was just stepping out of the shower when the telephone rang. She wrapped the velour bath sheet around herself and picked up the cordless telephone on the dressing table.

"Hello?" she said a little breathlessly, pushing a strand of wet hair out of her eyes.

A slightly muffled voice inquired, "Kit?"

"Is that you, Strong?"

"No, girl, it ain't Strong," the caller said ungrammatically.

She went very still. "Who is this?"

"No need for you to know who 'tis."

"If you don't tell me who you are, I'm going to

hang up," she stated, standing very erect, clutching the thick towel to her breasts.

"I wouldn't do that if I was you, girl." The threat was implied, but it was clearly a threat nonetheless. "You got my note?"

"Your note?"

There was a wheezing, asthmatic sound. "'The past will come back to haunt you, Mrs. O'Kelly.'"

"It was *you,*" she breathed through her teeth.

"Yup, it were me."

Kit slowly sank down on the cushioned bench in front of the vanity. "What do you want?"

The voice that was neither masculine nor feminine answered, "You'll find out soon enough. If you do like you're told nobody gets hurt. Understand?"

She inhaled a deep, trembling breath. "I understand."

"Do you read your Bible?"

"Sometimes." Her tongue was thick in her mouth.

"Even the Good Book says the sins of the fathers are visited upon their children."

Kit tried to follow the caller's ramblings, tried to humor him. *Or her.* She still couldn't tell if the voice on the other end was male or female. "Does it?"

"Yes, indeedy." There was a pause. "O'Kelly owes me. Owes a lot of people."

"Owes you what?"

There was an androgynous cackle. "All in good time. You'll find out all in good time."

Unshed tears burned Kit's eyes. "Please, won't you leave us alone."

"Can't do that, girl."

"Why not?" she asked in a half whisper.

"I finally want what's rightfully mine. You got to get it for me."

"Why me?"

There was no explanation forthcoming, just an insistent, "You're the only one who can."

Kit attempted to maintain her composure, but it was becoming increasingly difficult. "I don't understand," she cried out in frustration.

"You will."

"When?"

"Soon."

Then there was only silence. It stretched on for a minute, perhaps longer.

Kit swallowed and spoke hoarsely. "Are you still there?"

"Yup. Been thinkin'. Been thinkin'. Maybe it's time you and your man went on a second honeymoon."

"A second honeymoon?" she repeated. She couldn't have heard correctly.

"You heard me."

"But—"

"No buts." There was a pause, then a sharp, "You listenin', girl?"

"I'm listening."

"You give Strong a message."

Kit St. Clair sank her teeth into her bottom lip to keep it from trembling. She tasted blood on her tongue. It vaguely registered in the back of her mind that the blood was her own. "All right."

"Tell Strong he always was a lucky cuss." There was a fit of coughing.

She agreed. "I will."

"You got that?" came the gravelly voice.

"Yes."

"You use those exact words."

" 'Tell Strong he always was a lucky cuss,' " she recited verbatim. "What does it mean?"

"Strong will know. He'll figure it out. You be with him when he does."

"I don't see how I can be—" she began to protest.

Click.

"Hello? Hello, are you still there?" Kit spoke into the mouthpiece.

There was no response. Then she heard a dial tone. The caller had hung up on her.

She set the telephone back on the dressing table and stared, unseeing, into the vanity mirror. Then she picked up a wide-toothed comb and began to work through the tangles of wet hair left from her shower.

Strong.

His words from that very afternoon came to her. *"Take no chances. Watch your back. Call me if anything unusual happens. And I do mean anything."*

"I will."

"You have to promise, Kit."

"I promise."

Kit tossed the comb down and ran into the adjoining bedroom. She picked up her leather handbag and unceremoniously dumped the contents out onto the bed.

"Where in the world is it?" she muttered to herself as she frantically searched through her belongings. "What did I do with the darn thing?"

Her wallet.

There it was.

Strong's business card.

Flipping it over, she read the name of the motel and the local number he had scribbled on the reverse.

Kit plunked herself down on the edge of the bed, picked up the telephone on the nightstand and began to punch in the numbers. Her hands were shaking so badly that she had to stop twice and start all over again. She finally got it right on the third try.

He answered on the third ring. "Hello?"

"Did I wake you up?"

"No. I was stretched out on the bed watching the news." Strong absentmindedly rubbed his hand back and forth across his bare chest. "Kit?"

"Yes."

"You sound—odd." He pushed himself up into a half-sitting position and propped a pillow behind his head. "Are you okay?"

"Am I okay?" she repeated in a curiously blank voice. "A little scared maybe."

He shot straight up, pushed the pillow aside and swung his legs over the edge of the mattress. "Scared?"

"A little."

"What's happened?" he demanded to know.

Her breathing was labored and slightly erratic. "I received a telephone call."

"When?"

"A few minutes ago."

"Who was it?"

"He or she didn't say."

"You couldn't tell if it was a man or a woman?"

"No. The voice was muffled."

"Probably held something, maybe a handkerchief, over the mouthpiece," he deduced.

"The caller gave me a message—" he could hear Kit's voice quaver "—for you."

"Don't cry, Kit."

"I'm not crying."

Strong could tell she was. He'd always been able to tell. In a single motion he was on his feet and reaching for his jeans and boots. "I'll be right over. Give me your address."

She told him.

"Is your security system on?"

"Yes."

"Keep it turned on until you're positive it's me at the front door. Understand?"

"I understand."

"I should be at your house in twenty minutes."

"Thank you, Strong," she said, and he could hear her voice crack a little when she said his name.

"I'm on my way."

He hung up the receiver, finished pulling on his boots, tugged a plain white T-shirt over his head and stalked out the door of his motel room. He climbed into the Jeep parked outside, revved up the engine and took off down the otherwise quiet side street.

A wave of impotent fury swept through Strong. The message was for him. He knew that now. Yet the caller had made sure it was delivered through Kit.

"Sonofabitch," he swore, his eyes narrowed, his expression grim.

Katherine St. Clair still brought out some very primitive instincts in him, Strong realized as he turned down an alleyway that would cut five minutes off his time. She needed him to protect her, and, by God, that was exactly what he intended to do.

Starting now.

Starting tonight.

He would do whatever it took to keep Kit safe.

Seven

—

Kit was watching out the window of her Paradise Valley home when Strong pulled into the driveway, exactly fifteen minutes after she'd hung up the telephone. He climbed down from his dusty Jeep, slammed the vehicle door shut behind him and hurried toward the entrance of the house.

Kit had never been so glad to see anyone in her whole life!

She quickly entered the code to disarm the security system and ran to let him in. She opened the front door and Strong swept into the vestibule.

The first words out of his mouth were, "You look like you could use a drink. I know I need one."

"The bar is through there," she said, gesturing toward the rear of the dwelling.

"Got any beer?"

"In the kitchen. It's this way." Kit turned and headed in the opposite direction. He followed her.

The kitchen was a unique combination of modern appliances and southwestern-style Spanish architecture. The floor and countertops were done in an unglazed Mexican tile. The ceiling was raised and beamed with natural vigas—large, unfinished logs that served as supports for the roof.

The furniture was authentic, antique, primitive. There was a huge rustic cupboard against one wall, and in the center of the room a large table and four chairs.

"Sit," Strong commanded, placing his hands firmly on her shoulders until she sank into the nearest chair. "I'll serve." He opened the restaurant-size refrigerator and peered in at its contents. "Wine?"

She nodded. "Please."

Strong poured her a glass and set it down in front of her on the table. He helped himself to a can of beer and took a seat. He flipped the tab on the top, raised the can to his mouth, and took a long swallow.

They drank in silence for several minutes.

Then he looked right at her. Kit found his eyes unavoidable.

"Do you think you're ready to talk about it?" he finally said.

She fingered the delicate crystal stem of her wineglass. "I think so."

His voice was quiet but determined. "Would it help if I started out by asking a few questions?"

She swallowed and nodded.

"Did the caller know your name?"

"Yes."

"Exactly how did he refer to you?"

"As Kit. Several times as 'girl.' Once as Mrs. O'Kelly."

"You told me on the phone that you couldn't tell if it was a man or a woman."

"I couldn't tell," she repeated with weary emphasis.

"Was the voice young or old?"

"Old."

"You're sure?"

Kit surprised herself by stating, "Yes, I'm sure."

Strong sat back in his chair and inquired nonchalantly, "Would you say the caller's speech was educated?"

"No. It wasn't. In fact, I specifically recall that he—or she—used 'ain't' and dropped the endings of certain words."

Strong reached across the table and patted her hand. "Good girl. You'd make an excellent witness."

She gave him a watery smile. "Thanks."

He went on. "Was there anything—any noise on the line, any sounds in the background—that might indicate if the call was local or long distance?"

Kit closed her eyes and tried to remember. Nothing came. She shook her head.

"It's okay," Strong reassured her.

"There was something wrong with the person's breathing," she told him. "It had a kind of whistling, wheezing sound."

He frowned. "Like an asthmatic?"

"Yes," she said triumphantly.

Strong refilled her wineglass before they continued. Kit was feeling quite relaxed when he suggested that she tell him the rest of the story.

She did.

When she got to the end, the man sitting across from her checked and then double-checked the facts. He asked once more, "Are you positive that's what was said?"

"Positive." She repeated the important parts of the conversation for good measure. "First, there was something about the sins of the fathers are visited upon their children. Then the caller said, 'O'Kelly owes me...maybe it's time you and your man went on a second honeymoon...tell Strong he always was a lucky cuss.'"

"A lucky cuss—?"

"I asked what it meant. The only answer given was 'Strong will know.'"

"Well, I don't know," he ground out between his teeth.

"Whoever it was on the telephone tonight believed you'd figure it out," she said, her voice heavy with fatigue. "I'm supposed to be with you when you do."

"I could strangle the sonofa—" Strong paused, and seemed to reconsider his choice of words "—the sonofagun for getting you involved in this mess." The empty beer can was crushed in his bare fist. "I'm sorry, Kit. So damn sorry."

"You don't have to apologize. It's not your fault."

"I want you to know I'll take care of it," he said in a very hard, very dry tone. "Don't you worry."

"I'm not worried."

Well, maybe she was a little worried. But Strong didn't have to know that.

She attempted to make light of the situation. "I guess this lets Muffy Wainwright off the hook."

"Yeah, I guess it does at that." She could feel his eyes on her. "You look tired."

"I am."

"You'd better try to get some sleep." He pushed his chair back and got to his feet.

"I'll walk you to the door."

"There's no need."

"But—"

He cut in adroitly. "I'm not going anywhere, Kit. I'm staying here tonight."

She opened her mouth and shut it again.

"Won't you feel safer if I do?"

How could she respond both yes *and* no to the same question?

Strong pushed her for an answer. "Won't you?"

"Yes," she replied with what she hoped was a casual air, "I will feel safer."

"Then that settles it."

"The guest room is this way," she said. "The bed is already made up, and there are clean towels in the adjoining bath. You'll find anything else you might need in the cabinet next to the sink."

"Relax. You don't have to play the perfect hostess with me. I'll manage," Strong assured her.

There wasn't anything left for her to say but goodnight. So Kit did, adding, "I'll see you in the morning."

Strong turned off the lights in the guest room and stripped down to his jeans. He paced back and forth in the dark, then pushed the draperies aside and stood at the window looking out at the walled garden. It was filled with exotic fruit trees and swaying palms and lush flowers. There was a full moon tonight. He hadn't noticed until now.

A wraithlike figure appeared on the garden path.

It was Kit.

She was dressed in a long, flowing white robe and her hair hung down loose around her shoulders. She must have turned off the alarm in the back of the house. Anything was possible with these newfangled security systems.

He opened the sliding glass door in his bedroom and stepped outside. It was one of those perfect spring nights in Arizona—warm and wonderful, with a thousand—a million—stars twinkling overhead and the distinctive outline of the mountains in the distance.

The intoxicating fragrance of roses on the vine, cascading bougainvillea and flowering orange trees filled his nostrils. He seemed to remember another time and another place when the scent of orange blossoms had perfumed the air....

Like one of his ancient ancestors, Strongarm slipped silently through the night.

He wasn't stupid.

He wasn't crazy.

He wasn't a fool.

He certainly wasn't a glutton for punishment.

But curiosity, especially sexual curiosity, he was discovering, was a potent force.

Barefoot, and without a sound, he moved along the path toward the woman in white.

"I've always loved the scent of orange blossoms," Kit said without turning around.

She couldn't have heard him, yet somehow she had known he was there behind her. Strong wondered what had given him away.

"I remember you telling me that the first night we met," he said at last.

She faced him. "I did, didn't I?"

He shook his head and exclaimed with a small stoic laugh, "What a night that turned out to be."

"A night unlike any other," came the bittersweet admission.

Strong reached out and placed a single finger against her mouth. "Do you remember the first time we made love?"

He felt her tremble. "Yes."

He traced the outline of her lips. The upper first, then more slowly, more deliberately, the fuller bottom. "You were so damnably sweet," he murmured.

"And nervous," she confessed.

"A little. So was I."

"You seemed so self-assured, so confident."

"Appearances can be deceptive."

"Yes, they can be."

There was an underlying meaning to their words. They both understood that. In reality, he had been seventeen when they met, but big for his age, mature for his age, savvy, streetwise. She had been twenty-two, but when it came to experience, *she'd* been the child.

He looked intently into her eyes. "Do you remember the week we had together at the Stone House?"

She cried out softly, "Yes."

The heat was rapidly rising in his blood, but Strong didn't care. His body was swelling, thickening, but he ignored all the warning signs. "Haven't you wondered?"

"Wondered?"

"Was it as good as we remember? Half as good?" He dropped his hand to the pulse point at the base of her throat. He could feel the rapid rhythmic beat of her heart. Katherine St. Clair wasn't immune to him any more than he was to her. There was still something between them. Something powerful, something primitive. "Or have our memories played a dirty trick on us?"

Kit moved her head. It wasn't a definite yes or a definite no. "We were young. We were crazy. We thought we were in love."

He cut straight to the heart of the matter. "You were the best I ever had, sweetheart."

She pleaded, "Don't do this, Strong."

"Don't do what?"

"Don't torture me. Don't torture yourself. Let the past stay dead and buried."

"It's too late for that," he pointed out. "Somebody has already seen fit to raise the dead." He stared down into her beautiful face, illuminated as it was by moonlight. "I used to lay awake at night and tell myself you couldn't be as perfect as my mind said you were."

"Oh, God—"

"I dreamed of you night after night. I would wake up in a cold sweat, a hot sweat, my body in pain, aching for you, wanting you, needing you."

He felt her take two deep shuddering breaths. "Please—"

"Please *what?*" he whispered at her shoulder.

Tears welled at the edges of her eyelids. "Please leave me alone."

"Is that what you really want?"

Kit shook her head, and dug her fingernails into his arm. "Please kiss me."

Strong put his hands around her waist and brought her up tight against his body. Only her flimsy robe separated them. He could feel the sensual swell of her breasts, the hardened arousal of her nipples, the damp heat at the apex of her thighs.

"There is no past. There is no future. There is only the present, only this moment," Strong promised as he brought his mouth down on hers.

Eight

It was like the very first time.

Strong kissed her and she was no longer a rational, thinking, intelligent human being. Suddenly, within the space of a single heartbeat, Kit was a vulnerable, impressionable, unsophisticated girl again.

His hands—dear God, those incredibly wonderful hands—were around her waist, pulling her to him, holding her against him, anchoring her body to his.

It was *not* with a leisurely grace that his mouth moved over hers. He did *not* explore. He did *not* coax. He did *not* stop to savor. He did *not* linger over the smallest nuance of response he elicited from her.

He took.

He demanded.

He devoured.

He overwhelmed.

That quickly she was enflamed, impassioned, excited and afraid. She was all raw nerve endings and exposed flesh and bone. A tremor of sexual awareness shook her from head to toe. Her scalp tingled. Her skin was sensitized. Her breasts swelled. Her nipples became tender to the slightest touch, yet they itched to be caressed, to be squeezed, to be suckled, to be drawn deep into his mouth, to be nipped by his teeth in the pain that was pleasure.

Her stomach flopped over. Her knees buckled. Her blood boiled.

She was wild-eyed, half-hysterical, frantic and flustered. Her mind was muddled. She was disoriented. She had lost her equilibrium.

She was shaking like a leaf. She couldn't seem to breathe; she felt as if she was suffocating. She wanted to jump out of her skin.

He bewitched her. He becharmed her. He left her utterly bewildered.

She clung to him. She pushed him away.

She wanted to crawl inside his head, his heart, his very soul. She never wanted to see him again this side of hell. He was everything. She wanted nothing to do with him.

That's what it had been like when Kit was twenty-two. That's what it was like now that she was thirty-two.

Nothing had changed.

The man was dangerous. The man was lethal. She was putty in his hands.

"Damn you, Strong!" she cried out, half in agony, half in ecstasy.

"Damn you, Kit! I could almost break you in two," he growled, his fingers lightly encircling her throat. "I should have known better. I can't keep my hands off you."

"You never could," she challenged.

"No more than you could keep your hands off me," he shot back.

He was right. She had always loved touching him. She'd gloried in the feel of his smooth muscles, his hard angles and planes, the texture of his skin, the variances of his hair: the black, straight cut at his nape, the rough stubble of his beard the morning after, the soft crinkle of dark curls in which his manhood nestled.

He had fascinated her. She'd never tired of looking at him, touching him, kissing him, making love with him.

She wanted to kiss Strong now. Her way, not his. She made an impatient noise and went up on her tiptoes. Resting her hands on his muscular shoulders, she leaned toward him. His scent was fresh and clean and totally masculine. He smelled of plain soap, of hair still damp from the shower, of bare skin and faintly of leather.

She had always loved the way he smelled, the way he tasted, the way he felt.

A small sigh escaped her as she brushed her mouth back and forth across him. She did it a second time, allowing the tip of her tongue to moisten his lips, to slip quickly between them and skim the serrated edges of his teeth.

Strong groaned aloud. The sound began deep down in his chest and ended somewhere in the back of his throat. His arms tightened around her. He spread his legs slightly apart and urged her closer. She could feel his arousal straining at the confines of his jeans. His body reacted to the smallest movement on her part. It twitched, it throbbed, it pressed hard against her thigh.

Encouraged, Kit boldly delved into his mouth with her tongue. Her reward was to feel him shiver, to know that he was not immune to her, that she still had the power to drive him mad, quite mad.

It was at that point Strong apparently decided to take command. He plunged his arrowed tongue into her mouth, surged between her half-parted lips, ravishing, plundering, capturing. He was like a hot, scorching wind that tore the breath from her lungs.

Then Kit was vaguely aware that he had raised his hands to the fastenings of her robe. He undid half a dozen or more buttons from her neck to her navel before easing the silky material off her shoulders. He gently tugged the garment over her hips, and watched as it pooled into a soft, white puddle at her feet.

Strong's eyes slowly moved over her. The moonlight clearly revealed her breasts and their rosy centers. As he stared at her, she could feel the physical changes in her nipples. They grew, they hardened, they darkened, they became engorged. She wanted to cover herself, to shield her nudity from his view, but he would not allow it.

"Don't," was all he said.

"Why not?" she managed to ask after a minute, her voice coming out unintentionally low and husky.

"I want to look at you."

She didn't know what to say then except an urgently whispered, "I want to look at you, too."

The sinewy strength to Strong's long legs and lean thighs was evident even through the material of his well-washed jeans. It was a strength in perfect harmony with his muscular arms and broad chest. The taut lines of his abdomen emphasized the cloud of dark hair that arrowed down his body and disappeared into the waistband of his jeans.

"I want to touch you," she added, reaching out and daringly running her hand along his waist, across his flat belly and lower.

Her name was on his lips that quickly. "Oh, Kit, I want to touch you. I need to touch you."

He reached out and cupped her breasts, supporting their weight in his palms as his thumbs circled the rosy buds. He caressed first one, then the other. He caught them between thumb and finger, and gave each an erotic pinch.

Kit couldn't help herself. She put her head back and moaned with pleasure.

That was when he lowered his head and flicked his tongue back and forth from one pouting peak to the other. He nipped at her. He nibbled. He licked. He teased. He tugged. He drove her mad. Quite mad.

"I—I can't take any more," she whimpered.

That was when Strong finally took pity on her. He brought his lips to her breast once more and began to suckle, long and hard, pulling her deeper and deeper into his mouth.

This was crazy, Kit thought desperately. "Dear God, this is crazy!"

She didn't realize she had spoken out loud until Strong muttered in response, "It was crazy from the first moment, we both know that."

"Why did you come into the garden after me?" she inquired in a wild whisper.

"What makes you think I had any choice?" was all Strong said as he slid his hands down her body.

He began with the shape of her face, the outline of her nose, her ears, her chin. Then on to the long, slender length of her neck, her smooth shoulders, the inviting swell of her breasts, the firmness of her flat abdomen, the sensitive pubic bone, the soft, womanly mound that dipped between her legs.

He started again, this time at her nape and worked his way down her back, lingering over the small valley at the base of her spine, the curve of her hips, her rounded bottom.

He urged her closer and closer to his own growing urgency. She clutched at the waistband of his jeans and held on for dear life as he traced a sensuous line down the narrow fissure that divided her derriere.

Then his hand moved lower and he found her with the tip of his finger.

"Strong—"

He raised his head. His face was flushed. His green eyes glittered like two brilliant emeralds. "Do you like that, sweetheart?"

She could not think. She could not speak. She could not answer.

He probed again and her natural responses moistened his hand. He drove his finger into her farther and farther, until finally her body convulsed, and her soft cry of release broke the silence of the night.

At that instant his mouth came down on hers and he swallowed the sound of her climax. Simultaneously he lost control and she felt the shudders that racked his body.

It was like the very first time.

Ten years ago Strong had touched her, caressed her, and she had melted all over him.

It was just like the very first time.

Ten years ago she had innocently rubbed her body up against his, and he had exploded like a stick of dynamite.

"Nothing ever changes," murmured Kit, her lips numb, her mind empty, her body spent. She couldn't even raise her head from his shoulder.

"Some things never change," Strong agreed with a soft, self-deprecating laugh. "I have no self-control when it comes to you, lady. I never did. I never have." He sighed heavily. "I don't suppose I ever will."

He stooped to retrieve her robe. Slipping the flimsy garment over her head, he began to do up the buttons as if she were a helpless child.

"I can manage that," Kit insisted, but her hands and fingers wouldn't cooperate. She was all thumbs. In the end, he had to finish the job. "Thank you," she said politely.

"You're welcome."

Neither spoke for a minute or two.

Strong stood there in the moonlight, his dark hair mussed, his bare chest glistening with sweat, his face partially cloaked by shadows. He shrugged and did not even attempt to cover the telltale dampness on the front of his jeans. "I didn't mean for this to happen."

She focused on a point over his right shoulder where a palm tree swayed in the night air. "Neither did I."

"It caught me by surprise."

"Me, too," she admitted.

He made no move toward her. "Are you all right?"

How was she supposed to answer that question?

She had just allowed her ex-husband—for all intents and purposes, Strong was her ex-husband—incredible intimacies. She had kissed him like a woman starved for affection. She had touched him like a woman starved for sex. She had allowed him to kiss her, to touch her, to caress her, to bring her to a shattering climax.

How was she supposed to answer that question?

She was standing in the moonlight, her robe clinging to her body. Her skin was still damp from his lovemaking. Her breasts were swollen. Her nipples were tender and turgid. Her legs were wobbly. She wasn't even certain she could manage the few steps to her bedroom.

How was she supposed to answer that question?

What a ridiculous question under the circumstances, anyway.

Kit did the only thing she could. She lied. "Am I all right? Yes, I'm fine. Are you all right?"

Strong put his head back and gave a dark, sardonic laugh. "Am I all right?"

"That was the question."

"What the hell do you think? After ten years I've found I still can't keep my hands off you. I was all over you. I exploded in my jeans like an oversexed teenager. Oh, yeah, I'm fine. Just fine and dandy," he announced in a sarcastic tone.

"I'm sorry."

"About what?" Strong demanded to know. "About what we've just done?"

Kit tried to stay calm in the face of his anger. "Not about what we've just done. You said it yourself before we even kissed—for us there was no past, no future. There was only the present, only the moment."

"I know what I said," snapped Strong, failing to curb his irritation.

"I'm sorry you seem upset."

"I don't *seem* upset. I *am* upset."

Kit spoke softly, reasonably, as if to a small child. "You mustn't be too hard on yourself. The past few days have been particularly stressful for both of us. I suggest we chalk the whole thing up to experience, and try to get some sleep."

"Sleep?" he roared.

"It's getting late."

"It *is* late."

"I'm tired," she told him.

"I'm not surprised."

"We should call it a night."

"That's fine with me. Let's go to bed."

It was the way he said it. It was the look in his eye. Kit suddenly understood Strong meant go to bed *together.*

"No," she said simply.

"Yes."

"We can't."

"We can."

"It's not right."

"Why not? We're married."

She gave him a dirty look. "Not for long." She went on, "We would only be sorry in the morning."

Strong laughed and appeared vastly amused. "Speak for yourself."

Kit decided to try a different tack with him. "You know as well as I do that it's not logical for us to get involved with each other at this point."

He shrugged. "We were never logical, anyway."

She shook a finger at him reproachfully. "That was always one of our problems."

Strong backed off an inch, no more. "Katherine, you always could drive me crazy."

She planted her hands on her hips and stood her ground. "You drive me crazy, too. You have since day one."

"I was crazy about you," he drawled in a voice that made her heart beat double.

"Oh, no, you don't!" she tossed back at him. "You can't sweet-talk me, Strongarm Carlos Michael O'Kelly. I'm not the naive young girl you seduced ten years ago. I'm older and wiser now."

"You're older and wiser, are you? I suppose that explains the little episode in the garden tonight."

Kit blushed, a hot unstoppable blush right up to her ears. "I'm going to say good-night now."

He just stood there.

"Good night, Strong."

She was opening the sliding glass door to her bedroom when she heard a deep masculine voice mutter, "*Buenas noches,* sweetheart."

"Sweet dreams," she called softly over her shoulder.

Sweet dreams be damned.

Strong tossed and turned most of the night. It was toward morning before he drifted off into a restless sleep that was filled with faces from the past, people from the past, sins of the past.

The words went around and around in his head.

The past will come back to haunt you, O'Kelly.
Better wed than dead.
The sins of the fathers are visited upon their chil-

dren.
O'Kelly owes me. O'Kelly owes a lot of people.
Maybe it's time you and your man went on a sec-
ond honeymoon.
Tell strong he always was a lucky cuss.
Tell Strong he always was a lucky cuss.
Tell Strong he always was a lucky cuss.

It was after daybreak when Strong sat straight up in bed. It was coming back to him. Something Kit had said to him last night. Something someone had said to him a long time ago.

Somebody was playing games with them, all right. And he didn't like it. Not one bit. Not one damn bit.

It was time he explained the situation to Kit. She could be made to see reason. She would understand why she had to come back to the mountains and the Stone House with him. The answers were there. They just had to find them.

Maybe it was time for a second honeymoon, after all.

Nine

————

"**Y**ou want me to go *where* and do *what?*"

"Now, Kit—"

"Don't you 'now, Kit' me, Strong O'Kelly."

"If you would only allow me to explain," he said in his best attorney-at-law voice, making it sound as if *she* were being totally unreasonable when it was obvious, at least to her, that *he* was the one who had taken complete leave of his senses.

Kit paced back and forth in the living room of her Paradise Valley home, paused in front of the wall of windows that overlooked the sprawling valley below, and said, "Let's start from the beginning."

"An excellent idea," he concurred.

She gave him a long, measuring look. "Exactly when did this harebrained scheme occur to you?"

"Sometime during the night." Strong took a sip of the black coffee in his mug and reconsidered. "It may have been very early this morning."

"What first gave you the idea?"

He cleared his throat. "What was my inspiration?"

"If you prefer to think of it that way, yes, all right, what was your inspiration?"

He grinned. "Actually, you were."

"I was?"

"In a manner of speaking."

She tapped her foot impatiently on the natural wood floor. "In precisely what manner of speaking?"

Strong summed it up in one word. "Breasts."

"Breasts?" she hooted.

He nodded enthusiastically and set his coffee mug down on the table situated between twin antique Mexican love seats. "I was thinking about your breasts."

Kit threw up her hands.

"Okay, I was dreaming about them."

"This is the way the mind of a supposedly brilliant and up-and-coming young lawyer works?"

"No," he shot back, "this is the way the mind of a sexually frustrated man works."

"A fine line of distinction," Kit pointed out.

Strong thrust his hands into the pockets of his jeans and planted himself squarely in front of her. "Seriously, I believe I have a clue."

"That's more than I can say for most men," Kit muttered under her breath.

He gave her a long, hard look. "I want you to pay close attention and follow my line of reasoning."

She sunk her teeth into her tongue. "I'll try," she finally said with a deadpan expression.

He began. "After we went our separate ways last night, I found I couldn't get to sleep. So I was fantasizing about... I was thinking about... I was analyzing your—"

Kit raised her eyebrows. "Yes—"

"—Assets and liabilities."

"How very jurisprudential of you," she said dryly.

Strong picked up the thread of their conversation and continued. "The next thing I knew, I was picturing mountains in my mind."

"I assume I should take that as a compliment," Kit remarked in an aside.

"Absolutely," he assured her.

"I must have dozed off and on after that because the rest of it is disjointed, sometimes no more than bits and pieces—a face, an impression, a snatch of memory, a word or two."

She knew what he meant. "It can be like that when you aren't sleeping soundly."

Strong took his hands out of his pockets, folded his arms across his chest and got a faraway expression in his eyes. "I was up in the mountains with my great-grandmother. Rainbow Woman was very old by then, but there was a favorite place she wanted to see once more before she died."

Kit felt the sudden sting of tears at the back of her eyes.

Strongarm went on with his dream story. "It began to rain. Then the sun broke through the clouds and a rainbow appeared on the horizon. We sat together on the mountaintop and watched the *arco iris*. I remember she was very happy."

"How old were you at the time?" was quietly asked.

"Seven. Maybe eight."

"Your great-grandmother must have been an extraordinary woman," said Kit with respect.

"She was," Strong agreed. His eyes cleared and he became matter-of-fact again. "It turned out to be the last day we spent alone together. She died a short time later."

"I'm sorry."

He shrugged his shoulders. "It is the same for all of us. We are born. We live. We die," he stated philosophically. "Anyway, I must have had rainbows on the brain because I started dreaming about that old sonofagun Michael O'Kelly."

She was all ears. "Your paternal grandfather? The one you inherited the Stone House from?"

He expelled a breath of indulgent laughter. "The very one."

She smiled, remembering the stories she had been told about the colorful Irishman. "He must have been a character."

"To put it mildly." Strong shook his handsome head from side to side. "Pap certainly had the gift of the blarney."

"I suppose that explains your—" She made a light, airy gesture with her hands.

"Smiling Irish eyes?" he supplied.

"Yes, your smiling Irish eyes," said Kit, with more than a suspicion of amusement in her voice.

"I thought that's what you were going to say."

She wisely changed the subject. "Your grandfather was a miner, wasn't he?"

"Yup. In those days the miners mostly came from Cornwall to work the copper mines down in Bisbee. But not Michael O'Kelly. He always saw the pot of gold at the end of the rainbow."

"A dreamer."

"If there ever was one." Strong opened his arms and let them fall again in a classic gesture of futility. "Pap believed every damn story, every crazy tale, he had ever heard about buried vaults of gold bars, secret caches of coins and jewels plundered from the Spaniards and the church, veins of ore with nuggets the size of turkey eggs, rivers of silver that ran from the Arizona mountains all the way down to Mexico, the mother lode of the Lost Dutchman's Mine somewhere in those distant peaks," he said, pointing to the Superstition Mountains they could see on the horizon.

"There are still tourists and get-rich schemers who get lost every year in the Superstitions," she remarked. "There will always be people who look for the pot of gold at the end of the rainbow."

"Well, Pap was one of them."

"Did he ever give up?"

Strong shook his head. "He headed north to Prescott, met my grandmother and married her. They moved into an old stone cabin that used to be a stagecoach stop."

"The Stone House."

"My grandfather went right on searching for rainbows until the day he died."

"That was the year before we met."

"Yup."

Kit knew there had to be a point to the story.

"And that's when I remembered!" declared Strong.

"Remembered what?" she asked, shifting her weight from one foot to the other.

"It must have been in the back of my mind all this time." He picked up his mug, took a long swallow of coffee and set it down again.

Kit's excitement was mounting. "Yes—?"

"I just hadn't thought about it in so many years."

She was bursting with curiosity. "About *what?*"

"It was something your mystery caller said that must have acted as a catalyst."

"Acted as a catalyst," she prompted.

He quoted, " 'Tell Strong he always was a lucky cuss.' "

Kit clapped her hands together with delight. "He did say you'd figure it out. Tell me." She couldn't stand the suspense for one more minute. "What does it mean?"

Green eyes glittered in the morning light. "There's an old ghost town up in the mountains not far from Prescott and the Stone House."

"And—?"

"The name of the town is—or *was,* anyway—Lucky Cuss."

"I can't believe I let you talk me into this," Kit was still grousing several hours later as they loaded her suitcase into the back of his Jeep.

"It's only for one week," Strong pointed out for the umpteenth time. "The answers are there. We just have to find them."

She knew he was right. Still . . .

"I'm a successful businesswoman with a successful business to run," she reminded him.

"I thought Sally Bradford was a Phi Beta Kappa or something."

"She is."

"Then let her run things."

Kit sighed. "It's not the same."

Strong casually hooked a thumb through the belt loop of his jeans, pushed the Stetson back on his forehead an inch or two and squinted at her in the bright afternoon sunlight. "What in the hell do you do about your successful business when you want to take a vacation?"

"I don't take vacations."

"About time, then, I'd say."

She glared at him from behind her designer sunglasses, and resisted the urge to stick out her tongue. "And when was the last time you took a vacation?"

He grunted. "That's different."

"When?"

"All right, I admit it's been a while." Strong circled the dusty vehicle and gave each tire a healthy kick with the toe of his boot.

Kit followed in his footsteps. "What are you doing?"

"Testing the tires."

"With your gift for stating the obvious, I'll bet you don't lose many court cases."

"Not many," he said.

Somehow she believed him.

"Ready to go?"

"As ready as I'll ever be," Kit responded as she climbed up into the Jeep. Her handbag was slung over one shoulder and a large leather case over the other.

"What's all that stuff?"

"All that 'stuff,' as you put it, is my stock-in-trade—cameras, lenses, film."

Strong shook his head and laughed lightly under his breath. "Yup, I seem to remember you were always lugging a camera around with you."

"I like to be prepared. You never know when the next really big shot will be staring you right in the face," she told him as he turned the key in the ignition. Strong put the Jeep into reverse and backed out of her driveway.

"The next really big shot, huh?"

"I always have a camera handy."

He pulled his hat down partway over his eyes and said with a perfectly straight face, "I'll have to remember that the next time I strip down and head buck naked for the shower."

Ten

Before Strong opened the door of his office, he lowered his voice and confided, "Don't worry. Mildred Leeper is sweet, kind and the soul of discretion."

Kit pushed her hair back off her shoulders—she'd started wearing it down again for some reason—and said, "Ah, Mildred Leeper, your inimitable secretary and right hand. The one who, I believe you said, was old enough to be your mother."

"Actually I said she was old enough to be my grandmother. That may have been a slight exaggeration."

Kit's eyes narrowed behind the tinted glasses. She slipped them off and tucked them into her handbag. "What do you consider a slight exaggeration?"

The handsome man beside her showed his white teeth in a smile. "Don't tell me you're jealous?"

"Don't be absurd," she countered with all the composure she could muster. She hadn't expected Strong to read her mind quite so easily. "How long has Mildred worked for you?"

"About a year, give or take a couple of weeks." He leaned over, caught her chin in his hand, and kissed her hard on the mouth. "Before that, she was Clarence T. Martin's secretary and right hand for thirty years." He indicated the other name beside his on the door, turned the brass knob and called out cheerfully as they entered the office, "Good afternoon, Mildred. How are you today?"

A gray-haired, matronly woman glanced up from her work and, without preamble, rattled off, "There are a dozen urgent telephone messages on your desk, and a stack of mail two feet high that has to be dealt with before five o'clock. Judge Peterson wants to see you first thing Thursday morning in his chambers. Mrs. Lund called. She and the mayor expect you for dinner on Friday." She finally took a breath and responded, with a twinkle in her shrewd eyes, "I'm fine, thank you. How are you, Strong?"

The young attorney made a conciliatory gesture between the two women. "Mildred Leeper, Katherine St. Clair."

The usual formalities ensued.

"Hello."

"I'm pleased to meet you."

Strong stared at the door to his private office, then glanced back at Kit. "Can you give me an hour to deal with the worst of it?"

"Of course. Take as much time as you need. I'm very good at amusing myself," she assured him.

Business before pleasure was a fact of life that she, as the daughter of Matthew St. Clair and as a successful entrepreneur in her own right, had always understood.

"Thanks, sweetheart." He dropped a quick kiss on her lips. "I won't be any longer than absolutely necessary."

Kit watched him disappear through the connecting doorway. She was going to have to talk to Strong about his casual use of endearments, and about the proprietary habit he seemed to have fallen back into at the drop of a cowboy hat.

"Katherine St. Clair," repeated Mildred Leeper as she stood, put her shoulders back—although her posture was already ramrod straight—and came around to the front of her desk. "Would that happen to be the St. Clairs of Phoenix and Palm Springs?"

Kit sighed and confessed, "It would."

"I see."

There was a wealth of meaning contained in those two simple words. Mildred Leeper was obviously very fond of Strong. She apparently felt it was her duty to look after him, to take care of him, to protect him.

Kit looked the older woman right in the eye, and laid her cards on the table. "Strong has assured me you are the soul of discretion."

The slightest hint of color crept up onto the un-powdered cheekbones. "Humph. Got to be. I know everybody in this town and everything about them."

Kit took in a deep breath and slowly let it out again. "I'm Strong's wife."

There wasn't so much as the blink of an eyelash.

She revised her original statement. "I *was* Strong's wife."

In a perfectly reasonable tone of voice, the legal secretary inquired, "Which is it, dear?"

"It's a long story." Kit sighed, and sank down into a chair usually reserved for waiting clients. "We've been separated for a while."

"Awhile?"

"Ten years."

Mildred Leeper removed her bifocals, reached be-hind her for a tissue, methodically wiped off the lenses of her eyeglasses, and replaced them before com-menting, "Well, that does explain a few things."

"We were very young."

"I dare say, you're both still young." The sexage-narian continued with a trace of amusement in her voice, "Of course, at my age everyone seems young." After a moment she made a suggestion. "I think a nice cup of tea would be in order, don't you?"

"I would love a cup of tea!" Kit replied enthusias-tically.

It was some time later, after a second and third cup of tea and a plate of homemade cookies, that Mildred Leeper remarked to her, "Strong has never had much time for women. Now I understand why."

"Oh, but—"

There was no-nonsense air about the aging spinster when she stated, "You don't need me to tell you that you're a beautiful woman, Katherine St. Clair. You're the kind of woman a man doesn't forget. Leastwise not a man like Strong."

"I have never forgotten him, either," Kit said in a low, earnest voice.

"I'm relieved to hear that. Strong O'Kelly has always worked hard. Twice as hard as anyone else. He's driven himself day and night, trying to prove himself worthy."

"Trying to prove himself worthy of what?"

Mildred Leeper arched one slate-gray eyebrow. "Trying to prove he was worthy of being married to a St. Clair, for one thing." She gave a decisive nod of her head. "A formidable task even for a man of Strong's talents. He's a mighty fine man, you know."

"I know."

"I have only known one better."

"Clarence T. Martin."

Mildred nodded. "Clarence T. Martin, may his soul rest in peace."

When Strong came out of his office nearly two hours later he found his wife and his secretary having a cup of tea and gabbing like old friends.

"At least one of us is getting some work done around here," he teased.

"Kit and I have been having ourselves a little chat," explained Mildred.

He was curious. "A little chat about what?"

"It was girl talk," his secretary informed him, "and none of your business."

Strong's mouth dropped open. Girl talk? Mildred Leeper?

He knew who was behind this kind of female insurrection: Kit St. Clair. She had been in town for a total of two hours and was already turning his well-ordered existence upside down. Even his secretary was sassing him.

He wouldn't have it.

Strong turned on his heel one hundred and eighty degrees and glared at his wife. "Katherine?"

"Yes, darling," she said, looking up at him with an innocent expression on her beautiful face.

"I, ah . . ." He forgot what he was going to say.

His secretary took a step toward him. "You were undoubtedly going to give me those letters to type and get in the mail this afternoon." She was referring to the papers he clutched in his hand.

"Yes, if you would, please." Strong collected his thoughts. "I've returned the calls that were truly urgent. I've dealt with most of the important mail. Judge Peterson has agreed to postpone our meeting in his chambers until next week. I informed Mrs. Lund of my regrets since I have an unexpected guest staying with me." He glanced at Kit and shrugged his shoulders. "The mayor and his wife will be expecting both of us for dinner on Friday."

"I haven't a thing to wear," she said.

"There's a lovely little dress shop just down the street," piped up Mildred. "You must be about a size—"

"Eight."

"You'll have lots to choose from, then. With your coloring anything from bright yellow to vivid turquoise must look good on you."

His life was no longer his own, realized Strong. Not to mention his office.

He raised his voice to a level guaranteed to get their attention. "Kit and I have some important personal business to see to during the next several days. I won't be in the office much, Mildred."

The woman reached out and gave his arm a maternal pat. "I understand. I'll help in any way I can."

Strong was genuinely grateful to her. "Hold down the fort here, will you?"

Mildred Leeper snapped to attention. "To the last man. Or should I say to the last woman?"

He let it pass.

He had more important matters on his mind.

"I didn't want to say anything in front of Mildred but there was another anonymous note in my mail today," he informed Kit as he took her by the elbow and steered her toward the Jeep.

He could feel the cheerfulness drain out of her. "What did it say?"

Strong opened the door of the vehicle and settled her in the passenger seat. He went around to the driver's side and got in. It was only then that he reached into his breast pocket and removed the envelope.

"I don't want you to be afraid."

"I wasn't until you said that."

"No matter what it takes, I will protect you, Kit."

"I know that."

"With my life, if necessary."

She looked at him and he saw the tears well up at the edges of her eyelids. "What does the note say?" she asked in a husky voice.

He had to prepare her. He couldn't just spring it on her without any warning. "It's not just a note this time."

"What is it?"

"A photograph."

"A photograph of what?"

"Not of *what*. Of *who*."

"Of who?"

He swallowed. "Me." He opened the envelope and took out the enclosed snapshot. "There's some writing scribbled on the back," he said.

"Tell me what it says."

"All right." He took a deep breath and began to read aloud, " 'If a picture is worth a thousand words, then the other half of this one must be worth a million bucks to you, O'Kelly.' "

"Let me see it," Kit insisted in a small, firm voice.

Strong held it out to her.

It was a snapshot from the old days. Half of a snapshot, anyway. It had been deliberately cut down the middle with a pair of dull scissors. What was left showed a young Strong standing in front of the Stone House, smiling for the camera, his arm around someone. That someone was missing, but they both knew who had been in the original picture with him.

It had been Kit.

Eleven

They drove out of historic downtown Prescott, headed up the mountainside, navigated four or five steep hairpin turns in a row and followed the dirt road that lead through the national forest.

There were towering sixty-foot pines on either side of the narrow trail, their distinctive fresh scent permeating the high country air. Thick underbrush obscured the view on the one hand, a stream of rushing water formed by the last heavy rainfall raced along on the other.

Kit rolled down the window on the passenger's side of the Jeep and stuck her head out. She inhaled deeply and exclaimed, "It's wonderful up here!"

She was too busy gazing at the landscape to see the indulgent smile on Strong's handsome face.

"Yes, it is wonderful," he agreed.

"I had forgotten how beautiful the forest is," she admitted in a wistful tone. "It's so different from the desert—so cool and clean and green."

"We've had a lot of rain this spring," Strong told her, as if that somehow explained everything.

Then they came around the last bend in the road and there, nestled among the thickest part of the forest, stood the Stone House.

"The Stone House," she said, catching the tip of her tongue between her teeth.

Nothing had changed.

At least at first glance Kit thought nothing *had* changed. The house was still a hodgepodge of styles and periods. It had begun as a single-room cabin, a local stopping-off place in the days of the stagecoach. Later, one owner after another had added onto the structure until it reached its present form: a sprawling two-story dwelling of more than three thousand square feet.

After the death of Michael O'Kelly's wife some twenty years before, the old man had lost interest in the place. Sadly the house and the surrounding land had been allowed to deteriorate. It was in need of extensive repairs by the time Strong had inherited the property.

When they'd honeymooned here almost ten years ago, the Stone House had barely been habitable. But they hadn't cared. They were young and they were in love. Any place was heaven on earth when you were young and in love.

Still, something had changed.

Kit realized that the scrub had been cleared away from the house, and the flagstone path leading up to the front door had been recobbled.

There was a fresh coat of white paint on the wood trim and the windowpanes sparkled in the late afternoon sun. The slate roof had been replaced on the main section of the house and the garage, as well as the masonry around the garden wall. There were even a few hardy spring flowers poking their heads up out of the soil.

"Does someone live here?" she inquired.

"Yes."

Her heart sank to her feet. Somehow she hadn't foreseen that possibility. She knew her disappointment was visible on her face. "Who?"

Strong reached out and squeezed her hand. "It's all right, Kit. I live here."

"You live here?" she repeated. Of course, now that she thought about it, it made sense. "How long?"

"I've been working on the place for two, maybe three years in my spare time, but I just moved in a few months ago." He pulled into the driveway. "I have to warn you, the renovations aren't complete. There is only one bedroom and a bath finished upstairs."

Kit didn't care. She couldn't wait to see what he had done to the house. She jumped out of the Jeep and was waiting at the front door by the time Strong got there with his key.

"Don't get your hopes up," he warned her, obviously trying to temper her enthusiasm. "Like I said, the house still needs a lot of restoration."

He turned the key in the lock, pushed open the heavy wooden door and stepped back to allow her to enter first.

"Oh, Strong, you've done wonders with the place!" she said in a hushed voice.

The original hardwood floors had been carefully cleaned and waxed, then covered with area rugs, mostly second-hand Persian carpets.

Where needed, the walls had been repaired and re-plastered. A pen-and-ink sketch of the house as it had appeared at the turn of the century hung in the entranceway. Several vintage photographs taken over the years and a reproduction of a Remington were arranged on the walls.

The yellow pine banister leading up to the second story had been restored and polished until it shone with a golden hue. The entranceway opened into the living room and just beyond into the dining room and kitchen.

The rooms were sparsely furnished. The furniture was an eclectic mixture of "early attic," bargain basement and auction finds. It was large, utilitarian and masculine. Like the man who lived here.

Strong stood behind her and ran a self-conscious hand through the hair at his nape. "I told you, it still needs a lot of work."

She turned, went up on her tiptoes and gave him a hug. "I think you've performed miracles."

He was obviously pleased with her response, but explained, "It takes me so damn long to get anything done. I only have an hour here, an hour there, usually on weekends, sometimes not at all."

"You've done a wonderful job, Strong."

"The house could use a woman's touch."

That was true, it could. Kit had to ask. "Why haven't you ever remarried, then?"

Strong scowled. "I am married, in case you'd forgotten."

"I meant—" This was awkward. "Why didn't you ever remarry before you found out about us?"

He seemed disinclined to explain his reasons, and merely stated, "Too busy."

"Too busy?"

"I had to concentrate on what I was doing."

"Which was?"

"Working. Studying. College. Graduate school. After I passed the bar, I joined Clarence's law practice. Eventually I took it over. I haven't had time for women."

She heard something else in his voice, something akin to bitterness. "And—?"

Strong stared at her for a long moment. "And I had already been through hell once before with a woman. I wasn't real eager to try it again." There was the faintest hint of scorn in his tone. "Why didn't *you* ever remarry? You must have had plenty of opportunities during the last ten years."

She set her handbag down on a sturdy, all-purpose table just inside the front door. "Not as many opportunities as you might think. Once you weed out the fortune hunters, the publicity seekers, the gigolos, the fast-talkers trying to get through to my father—'' she clicked them off, one after the other, on her fingers ''—there isn't much left.''

Strong didn't believe her. That was evident by the way he leaned forward from the waist, and by the skeptical expression on his face. ''What's the real reason?''

Kit swallowed and told him the truth. ''I've never found anyone else I wanted *that* way.''

Her answer seemed to make perfect sense to him. ''Me, either. I could never have brought another woman into this house. It was ours. Yours and mine.'' He reached out and gently caressed her cheek with the back of his hand. ''It was you, babe, or it was no one.''

Her eyes were huge and sad. ''Dear God, Strong, what have we done?''

''Ruined one another for any other man or woman.'' The conversation was getting too intense. He gave her a funny little smile and suggested, ''C'mon, I'll give you the nickel tour and show you the rest of the place.''

An hour later Kit had seen everything from top to bottom, from stem to stern, inside and out, including an orchard growing wild in the back acreage that Strong hadn't even begun to prune back yet.

''That's next year's project. I hope,'' he added, blowing out his breath. ''I don't know how I'm going to get to it. The house has to be finished first.''

"Don't you have any help?"

He shook his head. "Nope, I'm doing it all by myself. Oh, I had to hire an electrician to check the wiring, and a plumber to see to the plumbing, but otherwise I'm learning as I go. In fact," he said, opening the door between the breezeway and the garage, "this is my workshop."

Strong's workshop was nothing more than a shed that measured approximately twelve feet by fifteen. It was filled with scraps of lumber, old coffee cans overflowing with nails and screws, buckets of paint and wood stain, tables and chairs rescued from yard sales, toolboxes, discarded doorknobs, orange crates piled one on top of the other.

Kit had never seen so much stuff in one place. Obviously the man never threw anything away.

"This must be your workbench?" she ventured, running her hand along the only clear surface in the shed.

There was no response from Strong.

"Is this where you work?" she repeated a little louder.

Still, no response.

Kit turned and discovered Strong standing directly behind her. He was staring at a spot on the wall above the workbench where he hung his hammers and screwdrivers.

"What is it? What's wrong?"

"It's gone," he said without moving his lips.

"What's gone?"

He dug into his shirt pocket and brought out the anonymous letter and the mutilated photograph that had arrived in today's mail. Thinking out loud, he said, "I wondered where the sonofabitch got a snapshot of the two of us."

"Where?"

He pointed to a small, empty space underneath an ordinary thumbtack stuck into the wall. "I always kept an old picture of us above my workbench. It's not there now."

Kit leaned forward and made a closer inspection. There was a scrap of something—it could have been a piece of photographic paper—stuck under the thumbtack. She glanced down at the snapshot in Strong's hand. There was a tiny section of one corner missing.

"Somebody has been in here," he stated, his anger growing, his green eyes on fire.

"Are you sure?"

He nodded. "Somebody has trespassed on my private property. Somebody has sneaked into my workshop and stolen the picture of us right off the wall."

"Who was it?" she voiced aloud.

They both knew the question was purely rhetorical.

There was an underlying sense of rage in every word Strong spat out. "I have had enough. More than enough. I am fed up with playing games. I am sick and tired of the other guy always having it his way. That is not my style. It never has been. It never will be. It is time I took things into my own hands. It is time I took action."

Kit reached out and tentatively placed her hand on his. She could feel the tension in him. It ran up the back of his hand and into his forearm, across his muscular chest and throughout his entire body.

Strong was mad. Madder than hell.

An idea occurred to her. It was time to share it with him. "Whoever has been harassing us believes the answer is here at the Stone House. That's the reason it was suggested we take a second honeymoon. Where else would we go, but back to the place where we had spent our first week together?"

"Keep going," he urged her.

"The culprit couldn't get into the house to make a thorough search because you've been living here the last few months. For some reason he's only recently become interested in whatever it is he believes you owe him." She licked her lips. "You did say it was crucial to ask not only *why* but why *now.*"

Strong's fingers were gripping hers so tightly that he was cutting off her circulation. "I think you may be onto something, sweetheart."

Her cheeks were flushed with excitement. "You think it's here in the house, too, don't you?"

"It could be." Kit could almost hear the wheels turning in his head. "More important, what if this sonofabitch has the wrong O'Kelly?"

"The wrong O'Kelly?"

"What if it isn't *this* O'Kelly—" Strong jabbed a finger at himself "—who owes him anything?"

There was a second, maybe two, of utter silence. Then they burst out in unison, "Michael O'Kelly!"

Strong went on in a coldly analytical manner. "You told me that the caller was old, that the language was outdated, even a little old-fashioned. Wouldn't that point the finger at someone of another generation?"

"An older generation."

"Exactly." His eyes were two chips of green ice. "It was Pap who was always poking his nose around that old ghost town. It was Pap who was always looking for buried treasure, for the pot of gold at the end of the rainbow. It was Pap who folks always said was a lucky cuss."

"There must have been photographs, old letters, receipts, official papers, things like that. What happened to all of his stuff after your grandfather died?"

Strong thought. "When I was cleaning out the master bedroom I came across a couple of shoe boxes full of junk. I crammed it all into the back of a closet to get it out of the way until I had time to deal with it."

"Maybe it's time you and I took a look at those boxes of so-called junk," suggested Kit.

Something, some sixth sense, some gut instinct, told her they were on the right track. Something told her they would find the answers to a lot of questions in this old house.

Something told her that when they had the answers to the past, they would also have the answers to their future.

Twelve

—

"**I**'m going to go blind if I have to look at one more fuzzy photograph of my grandparents, or relatives I don't know, or a receipt for a 1949 pickup, or another for a '54 sedan, or the paid-in-full notices for every year of taxes Pap paid on this place," declared Strong. "I don't think Michael O'Kelly ever threw anything out."

Kit bit her tongue. Apparently being a pack rat was in the O'Kelly blood.

"These shoe boxes are filled with family history, with bits and pieces of people's lives," Kit said, as she studied the old photographs she was holding in her hand.

Strong groaned and stretched his arms high above his head. "Let's face it, Kit, my girl. This isn't getting us anywhere."

Without stopping to think, she reached out and started to massage his shoulders. "Tired?"

"Exhausted. Boy, does that feel good," he moaned with pleasure. "How about you? Tired?"

"A little." With a weary sigh, she said, "I'm afraid we've made an awful mess."

Paper of every size and description was littered over the living room floor. Not to mention stacks of yellowing newspapers, piles of photographs, miscellaneous and sundry items, articles, keepsakes, announcements, births, deaths, licenses from fishing to hunting, envelopes of every style and type. The resulting chaos covered the carpet.

A half-eaten pepperoni pizza was on the coffee table behind them. It was the only remotely edible thing Kit could find in the house. Strong was a man of limited culinary abilities. The choices for tonight's evening meal had been either frozen pizza or canned ravioli.

At the time, the frozen pepperoni pizza had seemed the lesser of two evils.

He stifled a yawn and mentioned, "There is one more box."

Kit managed not to groan. "Where?"

"At the top of the stairs. Behind a trapdoor."

"Behind a trapdoor?"

Strong apparently felt it was necessary to explain. "It was originally built as a hiding place, or a secret storage area. Are you game for looking at one more box, or would you prefer to save it for another day?''

Kit was tired.

Dead tired.

But she had also enjoyed every moment of this evening with Strong. They had laughed together over silly photographs, shown each other some little item of interest they'd come across, exchanged a story or two, and sometimes simply shared a few minutes of companionable silence.

It was the kind of evening they had never had time for when they were young. They'd had one week together—a week of frenzied lovemaking. That had been the beginning and the end of their relationship.

She had loved the boy. Now she was discovering, ten years later, that she liked the man.

Kit bounced to her feet and, with more enthusiasm than she ever would have imagined possible under the circumstances, urged, ''I say we go for it.''

''I say we take a break and give each other a back rub—'' a deliciously wicked grin appeared on Strong's handsome face, his intent was unmistakable ''—or a *front* rub.''

''Business before pleasure, Mr. O'Kelly.'' She held out her hand to him. ''Let's go dig out that last box.''

Dig out was right. Five minutes later they found it under a thick layer of dust.

Strong coughed and attempted to wave away the thick gray air with his hand, complaining, ''Cripes, no one has opened this trapdoor in years.''

''You can say that again.''

"Cripes, no one has opened this trapdoor in years."

Kit gave him a swat on the backside, but that only raised another cloud of dust. They were both covered with soot by the time they hauled the box downstairs and wiped it off with a rag.

"Junk," Strong pronounced with disgust as he opened it up. "It's more damn junk. Broken pens. A rusting pocketknife. A jar of old pennies. Moldering books. Odds and ends. Hell, I don't even know what half of this stuff is. Junk. Junk. Junk." He threw his hands up in frustration.

"Now wait a minute," reasoned Kit. "Don't be so quick to judge. Here are some photographs."

"Great! Just what we need. More photographs. Photographs of people we don't know. Photographs of people we'll never know. Photographs of people we don't even *want* to know."

Kit ignored the tirade. "Here is your grandparents' marriage license. Their wedding album. Some legal documents. Hmm, a handwritten agreement . . ." Her voice trailed off.

Strong glanced up. "What?"

"This may be interesting."

"What is it?"

She paused for a fraction of a second before she said, "It appears to be a handwritten agreement of a partnership between three men who were friends. You'll no doubt understand what it is far better than I will."

Strong looked it over. "It is a partnership. Apparently one that Michael O'Kelly entered into with a couple of his cronies. They agreed to invest five hundred dollars a piece and, in turn, he was to work a mine called—"

Kit raised her head. "Called—?"

"The Lucky Cuss."

Her heart gave a leap. "As if that weren't enough proof, here is a photograph of your grandfather standing in front of what would appear to be The Lucky Cuss, itself."

She handed him a small, grainy, black-and-white snapshot of a young man, pick in one hand, shovel in the other, a broad grin on his handsome Irish face. He was standing at the entrance to a cave. There was a sign posted over his head with some kind of printing on it.

There was a peculiar outcropping of rock behind him on one side and a range of mountains in the distance. Otherwise, any distinguishing landmarks were few and far between.

Strong studied the picture. "Damn," he muttered, "I wish I had a magnifying glass."

"The photo is so small. It would help. Wait a minute!" Kit jumped up and ran into the next room. She returned with her camera bag. She opened it up and removed an expensive telephoto lens. "Let's see if this will work." She held it up to her eye. "Ah—"

"Ah, what?"

"See for yourself."

Strong peered through the lens. "Holy Moses!"

"Makes it nice and clear, doesn't it?"

"It certainly does. I can see every detail of Pap's face. He's a lot younger, but it is him." He put the lens down and turned the photograph over. "All it says on the back is June 1938."

"That's over fifty years ago."

Strong picked up the fragile handwritten piece of paper and studied it for a few minutes. "Basically the agreement was drawn up between Michael O'Kelly, Irishman and miner, and his two partners, Clester V. Rhodes and Arthur Moser. It states that on June 14, 1938, he accepted five hundred dollars from each man in order to buy the necessary supplies and equipment to work The Lucky Cuss. In exchange, the men agreed to split the profits from the mine in three equal shares."

Kit said matter-of-factly, "Surely the men who signed that agreement are all dead now."

"Dead or very, very old," Strong speculated. "I thought Lucky Cuss was the name of the ghost town but apparently it was the name of Pap's mine, as well."

Kit remembered something else, from her telephone conversation with the unknown caller. " 'Tell Strong he always was a lucky cuss.' " She tapped a finger against her bottom lip. "I wonder what kind of mine it was."

"It doesn't say. I take it back. It does. Kind of."

"Kind of?"

Strong peered at the tiny addendum at the bottom of the page. "There's a postscript signed by all three gentlemen. It says, 'Our word is as good as gold.' "

Kit's eyes grew as round as saucers. "They were partners in a gold mine!"

"That's the way it would appear."

"Did your grandfather ever mention the other two men to you?"

"Clester V. Rhodes and Arthur Moser? Nope, I've never heard of either of them. Of course, you have to remember Pap was old and frankly a little crazy by the time I knew him."

She tried to take everything into consideration. "Did he ever have any money?"

Strong laughed and shook his head sadly. "The man never had a dime to his name outside of this house, the five acres of land that surround it, and two hundred dollars in a savings account that was set aside to bury him. The two hundred didn't even cover the cost of a decent casket."

"Then Michael O'Kelly never struck it rich."

"That's for damn sure."

Kit clicked her tongue. "It doesn't make any sense. The caller said, 'O'Kelly owes me. O'Kelly owes a lot of people.' What could O'Kelly possibly owe him? Or anyone?"

"It beats me."

She snapped her fingers together. "Unless one of those old coots—or their heirs—is still alive and believes that Michael O'Kelly did strike it rich."

"What? And didn't tell them? Didn't share it with them?" Strong stretched his long legs out in front of him and rubbed a cramp in his thigh. "That doesn't make any sense." Then he gave a tired laugh and confessed, "Of course, if there's one thing I've learned in my three years as an attorney, it's that people often don't make any sense."

"How would we go about finding out if Clester V. Rhodes or Arthur Moser is still alive?"

He shrugged and suggested, "We could start with something simple. Check the local telephone directory."

She beamed at him. "You're brilliant."

"I know," he said immodestly.

Kit scampered into the kitchen and came back with the telephone book tucked under her arm. In less than two minutes she had her answer. "Neither man is listed in here."

"That doesn't tell us everything, however," Strong was quick to point out. "If they are alive, those men would have to be in their eighties. They could be living with their children. They could be in a nursing home. They could even have an unlisted telphone number. Or they might not have a telephone at all."

"Are you always this logical and thorough?"

"Always."

"Don't you ever stop thinking?"

Strong got a look in his eyes that Kit knew only too well. "Sure. Sometimes. With the proper incentive."

"Forget I asked that last question." Then she thought of something. "I know who we should ask about Clester V. Rhodes and Arthur Moser."

"Who?"

"Mildred Leeper."

"My Mildred?"

"Your Mildred. Just this afternoon she told me that she has to be the soul of discretion because she knows everybody in this town and everything about them."

Strong rubbed the stubble on his chin. "She has lived here all of her life."

"She worked for a leading attorney for more than thirty years," Kit chimed in.

"She's sharp as a whip. She never forgets a name or a face. I wouldn't trade her for ten lawyers."

"Mildred is our man!" Kit started to get to her feet. "Let's call and ask her right now."

Strong reached out, grabbed her by the arm and dragged her back down to the floor. "Whoa! We can't do that."

"Why not?"

He pointed to the clock on the wall. "The time."

She studied both hands on its face. "Two o'clock?"

"Yup."

"Two o'clock in the morning?"

He nodded. "Or two o'clock in the middle of the night, depending on your viewpoint."

"No wonder we're tired."

Strong yawned and struggled to his feet. "Do you want to take a shower before you go to bed?"

Kit took one look at her hands. They were filthy. "I think it's going to be an absolute necessity in my case."

"The bathroom is up the stairs, the first door on your right. There should be clean towels, soap, shampoo and anything else you need in the linen closet."

"I can manage. You don't have to play the perfect host with me."

"I'm going to put a few of these things away. I want those partnership papers and that photograph stashed somewhere safe for the night."

"I'm off, then," said Kit.

She didn't want to ask where she was supposed to sleep. She didn't want to ask where he intended to sleep. She did remember, however, that Strong had said only one bedroom and a bath upstairs were fit for human habitation.

He must have read her mind. "Take the bedroom next to the bath. I put your suitcase in there earlier. Let me know if you need anything—more hangers, another blanket, an extra pillow."

"Thanks, I'm sure I'll have plenty of everything."

She still wanted to know where Strong was going to sleep. Surely she could ask a simple question of him without getting embarrassed. After all, she was thirty-two years old. "Where will you sleep?"

The man was visibly exhausted, but he still got that little smile on his face and teased, "Is that an invitation?"

"Just curiosity."

"The living room sofa opens up into a double bed," he told her.

Her mouth formed an O. "Oh, I see."

"I thought you might."

"I guess I'll head for the shower, then."

"I will have to share a bathroom with you. It still has the only shower in the house that works. Don't worry, I'll give you plenty of time before I come up."

"Good night, Strong."

"Good night, Kit."

"I think we've really stumbled onto something important with this partnership and The Lucky Cuss," she called back to him over her shoulder.

"Tomorrow is another day."

She paused on the bottom step and said, frowning, "Who said that?"

Strong gave a little grunt that may have been a laugh. "I could have sworn I just did."

Strong came out of the shower, slipped into a pair of clean pajama bottoms, draped a towel around his neck and decided to see if Kit needed anything. He knocked lightly on the bedroom door. It wasn't closed all the way, and the pressure of his hand opened it even further.

The curtains were shut. The small lamp on the bedside table was still lit. He half expected to find her reading a book or sitting up in bed, her back propped up against a pile of pillows, eager to discuss what they had discovered.

Instead he found that she was fast asleep. He quietly moved across the master bedroom and sat down in the old-fashioned rocking chair and watched her.

God, she looked so young. She looked so much like the girl he had first fallen in love with. She looked so vulnerable, so in need of his protection.

Katherine St. Clair would like the world to think that she was strong, independent, capable, self-assured, coolly efficient, businesslike and always in control. That she didn't need anybody, or anything.

That was a bunch of bull.

Kit was a warm, sensitive, loving and lonely human being. She was also very possibly in danger, thanks to him.

Whatever the cost to himself, Strongarm Carlos Michael O'Kelly faced one bitter but honest truth: he would do whatever it took to keep his wife safe.

Kit wasn't certain what had awakened her. She lay there for a moment in the dark, not knowing where she was.

Then she remembered.

She was staying at the Stone House. She was with Strong. She was sleeping in his bed.

She could hear the birds twittering outside the window. It would soon be dawn. There was a pale gray light behind the curtains instead of the black of night.

She turned her head on the pillow.

That's when she saw him.

Strong was sitting in a rocking chair next to the bed, his head slumped to one side. He was wearing a pair of pajama bottoms and nothing else. His chest was bare. So were his feet. He must have gotten cold sometime in the night and pulled an old afghan over himself.

He was fast asleep.

He looked tired and uncomfortable. Part of her wanted to wake him up and tell him to come to bed, to stretch out his long body beside hers. It was ridiculous for her to have a king-size bed all to herself while a man six-four sat scrunched up in a chair too small for him.

Her heart went out to him.

As she watched him, Kit knew that for the rest of her life, for every single day from now until she breathed her last breath, she would love this man. It came as no surprise to her. He was the only man she had ever loved.

It had been love at first sight, too. She believed that with all her heart and soul. She had loved him when he was a boy and she was a girl. They'd had one week together in this house. One glorious week of love and laughter. Oh, God, how she had loved him then!

Dear God, how she loved him now.

The past will come back to haunt you, Mrs. O'Kelly.

This man was her past and her present. She just didn't know if he was her future.

Could they forgive each other and start anew? He had lied to her once and she would have to learn to trust him again. He believed that she hadn't loved him enough to stand by him when the chips were down. Could he learn to trust her again? Did he even still love her? There had not been one word said about love.

Oh, Strong wanted her. She knew that. But she didn't know if there was anything beyond wanting.

And sex was never enough.

Tears welled in her eyes. She shut them tightly and tried to will them away. She bit down on the edge of the sheet to stop the sound of her crying.

She heard her name being softly spoken. "Kit?"

She opened her eyes and discovered that Strong's eyes were also open. He was watching her.

She gulped and tried to speak. "G-good morning. It's almost morning anyway."

"Why are you crying?"

"Am I crying?" She reached up and used the back of her hand to wipe away the tears on her face. "How silly of me."

"You didn't answer my question."

"No. I didn't."

"Why won't you tell me?"

Because knowledge is power, she wanted to say. Because if a man knows how a woman feels about him he can use it to his own advantage, he can use it against her.

Because she was a coward. Because she was embarrassed to confess her feelings. Because she didn't want Strong to know that she still loved him.

His voice was soft, as soft as she had ever heard it when he said, "I never could stand to see you cry."

"Why?"

"Because it tore me apart inside. It still does," he admitted, pushing the afghan aside. He went down on his knees beside the bed, his elbows resting on the edge of the mattress. He reached out and tenderly wiped the remaining tears from her face with his fingertips.

"Strong—"

"When you cry, I cry. When you laugh, I laugh. When you're afraid, then I'm afraid for you. When you hurt, I feel the pain. When one day you die, that is the day I die, too."

Kit could not speak. She simply opened her arms to the man she loved and invited him into her bed.

Strong slipped his pajama bottoms down and stepped out of them. He was as God had made him when he joined her under the covers. His body was smooth and muscular and hard as nails.

Some things never changed.

Kit asked him no questions. He made her no promises. There was no yesterday. There was no tomorrow. There was only now. There was simply this man and this woman who needed each other, who wanted each other, who were starving for what the other could give, for what they would receive in return.

It was sex.

It was lust.

It was loving.

It was passion.

It was meeting of minds and bodies, of hearts and souls.

There were whispered words. There was silence. There was an understanding that went beyond any language.

Strong made love to her the first time in a fever, stripping the nightgown from her body, feeding upon her breasts as if he were a starving babe and she its mother with rich milk brimming from her nipples.

There was no foreplay. He parted her thighs. He thrust into her with a single motion, all the way in, up to the hilt. She was ready for him. She took him, every inch of him, all the way.

They did not bother to even separate before they started again. Strong rolled onto his back, taking her with him. Kit sat astride his wonderful body, her knees pressed to his sides, clinging to him wherever and whenever she could. She rode him as if he were a magnificent stallion.

Their flesh was passion-slick. Her hair grew damp and streamed over their bodies like wet silk. Her milky-white skin was flushed pink, her nipples ruby red. There were tiny scratch marks here and there on both of them, but neither gave it a second thought, neither cared a whit.

The morning sun was coming over the mountains and streaming into the east-facing window as they stretched out alongside each other and took time to luxuriate in their lovemaking. This time each nuance was appreciated. Each kiss, each caress, each response was given and received with loving attention. They had nearly ten years of dreams, of yearnings, of desires to make up for.

It was midday. The sun was already high in the sky when they finally awakened in each other's arms, and sighed, satiated.

"I wonder if I'll be able to get up," moaned Strong as he lay beside her.

Kit laughed lightly, softly, intimately. "I didn't notice it being one of your problems earlier."

He playfully tweaked her bare bottom. "I meant get up out of this bed. I swear every muscle in my body aches."

"Then I'll just have to kiss them better."

"Oh, no, you don't." Strong laughed, and it was a rich, deeply satisfied, masculine sound. "That's how I got into this shape in the first place." He arched a questioning brow in her direction. "You must have a sore muscle or two yourself."

"One or two," she groaned as she turned over in bed and tried to sit up. "You don't think we're too old for this, do you?" she asked, looking back at him over a bare shoulder.

"Are you kidding?" He laughed again. Then held his side where it hurt. "We're just a little out of practice."

"A little?"

"All right, a lot." He stood up and stretched. "You get the bathroom first. I'll make the coffee and call Mildred."

Kit looked at him as if he were crazy. "Call Mildred?"

"You said it yourself last night. She knows everything about everybody in this town and within a fifty-mile radius. I want some answers about Michael O'Kelly's former partners. I want this thing settled now."

She stood beside the bed, buck naked, and threw him a smart salute. "Yes sir!"

He quirked a dark eyebrow at her. "Have I ever told you how I deal with a sassy wife?"

Kit reached for her nightgown. It was in a heap on the bedroom floor. "Nope."

He groaned as he pulled on his jeans. "Remind me to show you sometime."

She was all wide-eyed innocence as she inquired, "Why not now?"

Strong gave her a look that clearly said she would pay for that comment later. "Let's just say, I'm not up for it."

Thirteen

"**R**emind me to give you a raise."

Kit walked into the kitchen later that morning as Strong was talking to Mildred Leeper on the telephone.

He laughed at something his secretary said. It was a wonderful sound that began deep down in his chest and bubbled up into his throat. Kit had always loved Strong's laugh.

"All right," he was saying to the matronly woman, "remind me to give you *another* raise. Thanks, Mildred, you're as good as gold." He listened for a minute. "No, Kit won't have time to go looking for a dress. You ladies will just have to do your shopping another day. We already have plans for this afternoon." He listened again. "Yes, I promise to tell her. No, I couldn't say when. We'll see you sometime tomorrow."

"You promise to tell me what?" Kit inquired the second he hung up the receiver.

Strong raised his eyes heavenward, indicating the need for patience. "Mildred has apparently been out perusing the dress shops in town. She said to tell you there is a stunning canary yellow in a size eight that's perfect for you."

"I adore canary yellow," she said.

"Then you'll be glad to hear that the store has agreed to hold the dress until five o'clock tomorrow."

"How kind of them," she said appreciatively.

"Yeah, like they don't know a sucker when they see one," he snickered.

She planted her hands on her hips and gave him one of "those" looks. "What is that supposed to mean?"

Strong muttered incredulously, "The price of the dress is six hundred damn dollars."

"So?"

"How many women in Prescott are going to rush out between now and tomorrow afternoon and buy a canary-yellow, six-hundred-dollar dress?"

On occasion, Kit had found, there were advantages to being a princess.

In a voice that had put more than one man in his place, she said, "I was unaware of the fact that you're an expert on the subject of shopping. Personally I don't know how many women in Prescott will rush out between now and tomorrow to buy a canary yellow dress for six hundred dollars. I do know it was very thoughtful of Mildred Leeper to take the time to find a dress for me. And it was very nice of the store to hold it until I have a chance to get into town." She looked down her aristocratic nose at him—no small feat when he was a good seven or eight inches taller than she was. "Don't you agree?"

Strong muttered, "I guess so." He was smart enough to change the subject as quickly as possible. "I see you're dressed and ready."

"Ready and raring to go," she assured him.

She was wearing jeans, a sweater, a pair of rugged hiking boots laced up to the ankles and a wide-brimmed, protective hat. Slung over her arm was a lightweight all-weather jacket, a water canteen, her camera paraphernalia and a packet or two of beef jerky. Personally she detested the stuff, but it seemed to be standard equipment in this part of the world when one was going out into the wilds.

Strong filled a mug with coffee and handed it to her, then poured another for himself. He leaned back against the kitchen counter and studied her over the rim of his cup. "Sometimes I forget how incredibly efficient you are."

"It's one reason I've been so successful. I run my business with the same efficiency," Kit told him briskly.

"I don't doubt that for a minute," he remarked.

Kit bestowed a smile upon him. She was feeling enormously pleased with herself this morning. Of course, it might have more to do with sexual satisfaction than efficiency. Nevertheless, she had more important things on her mind.

"Tell me, what did Mildred find out about your grandfather's former partners?"

Strong finished his coffee, rinsed out the cup and set it in the drain rack. "Are you ready for this?"

"Yes," she said, nodding her head vigorously.

"It turns out that Clester V. Rhodes, better known to his friends as 'Peg,' *and* Arthur 'Cactus' Moser are both alive and kicking."

Her mouth dropped open. "Both are still alive?"

"And kicking."

"Bless Mildred Leeper!" she exclaimed with wholehearted approval. "You really should give her a raise."

"The woman already makes more than I do," Strong informed her in a dry tone.

"Yes, but *she's* worth it."

He took a purposful step toward her. "Like I said, remind me to show you later how I deal with a sassy wife."

With a perfectly straight face, Kit couldn't resist the temptation to add one stipulation, "When you're feeling up to it."

His eyes darkened to a deep emerald green. "When I'm feeling up to it."

Kit was well aware that she playing with fire. But she had discovered something in the past several days. It was fun playing with fire. It was exciting. It was challenging. And it was very erotic when the man was Strong O'Kelly.

"Promises. Promises," she murmured under her breath.

"What did you say?"

"Problems. Problems. Knowing they're both still alive only solves one of our problems. I don't suppose she was able to get an address for either gentleman."

He arched a brow. "Even Mildred isn't that good."

Kit finished her coffee and, following her host's example, rinsed out the cup and set it upside down in the drain rack. "What do we do next?" she asked.

"We are going out into the wilds today."

She knew it! "I'm prepared."

"I can see that you are," Strong commented. He darted an odd look at the packages of beef jerky in her pocket. "Do you actually intend to eat that stuff?"

Kit wrinkled up her nose in distaste. "Only in an emergency, a dire emergency."

"So, nobody knows for sure where either man is."

"Rumor has it," Strong told her as he stowed their gear in the back of the Jeep, "that Cactus Moser has a girlfriend who lives over around Jasper."

"A girlfriend?" She snorted softly. "At his age?"

Strong couldn't resist. The form-fitting jeans Kit was wearing fit her to a T. They clung to her nicely rounded hips and derriere in a most provocative manner. He reached out and gave her backside a lingering pat. "Some of us are never too old to appreciate the opposite sex."

She opened the door on the passenger's side and hopped up into the Jeep. "You mean, the 'better sex,'" she said in a no-nonsense tone.

He settled a confounded expression on his face. "Better at what?"

"Navigating, for one thing," Kit told him in no uncertain terms when they turned off the dirt road and headed into open meadow twenty minutes later. "Are you sure you know where you're going?"

He took both hands off the steering wheel and shrugged, before returning them to the wheel. "Hey, the guy at the gas station said, 'Take the first left and follow the street signs. You can't miss it.'"

She gave him one of those exasperated looks he'd noticed women always did so well.

"Very funny," she said.

"God knows, I try," he claimed. Then he reached out and placed his hand on her knee for a moment. "Don't worry, Kit. I know where I'm going. I used to come up here all the time when I was a kid."

"I'm not worried."

"Good. You see, the way I figure it, since nobody seems to know the exact whereabouts of Peg Rhodes or Cactus Moser, we do the next best thing."

"Which is?"

"We locate the mine."

"The Lucky Cuss?"

"Yup."

He could almost see the light bulb switch on over her head. "You think the mine must be somewhere near the old ghost town, right?"

"Right." He glanced at her out of the corner of his eye. "You're a very bright woman."

She was absentmindedly chewing on her bottom lip. "I know." Something was obviously puzzling her. "How do we know where the mine is?"

"We don't."

She looked at him as if he were crazy. "Then how in the blue blazes do you think we're going to find it?"

"*We* aren't. *You* are."

"*I* am?"

"I have an idea. Please allow me to explain."

"I wish you would."

"You're a talented photographer."

"Thank you."

"You're an artist. You see the world through different eyes than the average person."

She impatiently drummed the dashboard. "Is this going to be another one of your incredibly long-winded, roundabout attorney-at-law-type stories?"

"Pay attention."

"Yes sir."

"In my pocket I have the snapshot we discovered last night of Michael O'Kelly posing in front of The Lucky Cuss."

"Hmm."

"You brought your camera and telephoto lens."

"Of course."

"When we reach the ghost town in a few minutes we are going to attempt to recreate the original photograph with me standing in for my grandfather."

Kit's mouth dropped to her chin. "*That* is your brilliant idea?"

Strong's hands tightened on the steering wheel. "I didn't say I had a brilliant idea. I never claimed it was brilliant. I simply said I had an idea."

"Excuse me. I stand corrected."

He scowled and thrust out his jaw. "Do you have a better idea?"

"No," she admitted. Then she allowed, "It might work. It could work." She threw her loose brown-to-blond hair back from her shoulders and adjusted the hat on her head. "Actually it's a very creative solution to an unusual problem."

"Thank you."

She shrugged. "Of course, it's a long shot."

"A long shot?" Strong repeated, a puzzled expression on his face. "That must be some kind of technical term you professional photographers use."

She laughed out loud. Then he joined her. They were still laughing when he expertly maneuvered the Jeep over the next hill and stopped.

"Here we are," he announced.

"Here we are?" Kit looked disappointed. "Where?"

"The town of Lucky Cuss."

"This is it?"

He was amused by her naiveté. "What did you expect? The back lot at a movie studio?"

"But there's nothing here but tall grass and a few rotting boards."

Strong stepped out of the Jeep, leaned his arm against the open window of the vehicle and gazed off toward the horizon. "Lucky Cuss is just like a thousand other ghost towns in the western United States. Hidden up in the hills, it's no more than a few old weathered buildings, a wagon with the wood rotting through, maybe some rusty nails and horseshoes lying around, or bits of colored glass and a long-forgotten cemetery, the markers blown over by the wind, the names and dates obscured, even erased, decades ago by the rain and the sun."

"What do you know about this particular town?" asked Kit, apparently interested in spite of herself.

Strong told her as much as he knew. "It was once a thriving little community that grew up around mining. The miners came first, of course. They pitched their tents and cooked on open fires and hunted for gold or silver, copper or mercury. Whatever precious metal they'd heard was hiding in the mountains, the rocks, the canyons."

"Somebody was always looking to strike it rich, weren't they?"

"If not the miners, then those who came after them—the camp followers."

Kit got out, tramped through the tall grass and circled the Jeep to stand beside him. "The camp followers?"

"The professional gamblers, the prostitutes, the cooks and barbers, laundrymen and storekeepers, thieves, maybe even a lawman or two. Sometimes if a boomtown lasted long enough, decent folks moved in and it became a real town with a school and a church. Civilization took over, then.'' Strong slipped an arm around her shoulders and tucked her into his side.

''Which kind of town was Lucky Cuss?''

''Somewhere in between boom and bust.''

''But it eventually died.''

He nodded. ''It eventually died. The past wasn't enough to keep it going. It was a ghost town long before either of us was born. I remember Pap brought me up here one time when I was just a boy. It was a derelict even then. It looked pretty much as it does now.''

She shivered.

''You cold?''

''No.''

''I can get your jacket.''

Kit shook her head. ''Somebody stepped on my grave, that's all.'' She looked up at him. ''Go on.''

''Let's walk. I'll show you.'' They moved a short distance away from the Jeep and he indicated some forty or fifty feet ahead of them. ''The grass has grown up in what used to be the main street.''

''That was the main street of a town?''

''Yup. You can see the few buildings that remain are no more than storefronts now. The houses are tumbledown shacks. There is even a piece of old lace curtain blowing in the window of that one.''

''What's that sound?''

"A sign swaying in the wind, it's creaking back and forth on a rusty chain. Strange places, ghost towns."

"You're giving me the willies."

"Don't worry. There isn't anything here to hurt you."

She tentatively smiled at him. "In that case, when do we get started?"

"Now."

They trudged back for their supplies and equipment.

Strong ran through his list. "One pair of binoculars. One compass. One shovel. One pick. One machete."

That stopped Kit dead in her tracks. "One machete? What in the world are you going to do with a machete?"

"Clear away the entrance to the mine if it's overgrown with vegetation."

"Now you're beginning to sound like my brother."

"What makes you say that?"

"He recently brought one of those big knives back from the Philippines. Apparently he'd used it to clear away vegetation in the jungle."

Strong gave a nod of understanding. "A machete can be a handy thing to have around." Ten minutes later he asked, "Are you ready?"

"As ready as I'll ever be."

With his big knife hanging at his side, Strong suggested, "Then let's get started."

* * *

"Brilliant idea, my—foot!" muttered Kit as she peered for the umpteenth time through the camera's telephoto lens. Strong was standing some distance away in front of an outcropping of rock.

The wrong outcropping of rock.

She cupped her mouth with her hands and yelled as loudly as she could in his direction, "No!"

He shrugged, picked up his load of mining equipment and pointed to a mound of earth, rock and stunted trees some fifty feet from his current location.

"Why not?" she grumbled. "One bunch of rocks is as good as another."

It wasn't that she was a spoilsport, Kit reminded herself. She had been a damn good sport...for the first three hours. But now she was hot and tired. Not to mention hungry and thirsty.

Her arms ached.

Her legs ached.

Her head ached.

Even her back ached.

And she seemed to have lost her sense of humor some three rock outcroppings back.

She glanced up and saw that Strong had positioned himself in front of the latest location. She raised the camera and peered through the telephoto lens. With a sigh of fatigue, she put it down again.

Then she raised it once more and took another look.

It couldn't be.

She dug into the pocket of her jeans and took out the small photograph of Michael O'Kelly posing in front of The Lucky Cuss. Then she held up her camera and studied Strong O'Kelly standing in front of a peculiar rock formation.

A somehow familiar rock formation.

"It might be," she murmured.

It could be.

It was.

She let the camera hang down between her breasts and called out to Strong as loudly as she could, "Yes!"

A faint echo came back to her, "Yes?"

She jumped in the air, nodded her head and yelled even louder, "Yes, that's it!"

Fourteen

"I told you a machete would come in handy," declared Strong as he swung at the thick vegetation covering the entrance to what they believed was The Lucky Cuss.

"Just be careful you don't chop off anything important," Kit warned him as he hacked away at fifty years' worth of scrub and underbrush.

"Don't worry, honey—" he glanced down at the front of his jeans "—I'm being careful."

Kit raised her eyes upward, reminding herself to be patient. Strong was a man in many ways, after all, like other men. "I meant fingers, toes, appendages."

Strong O'Kelly paused, wiped the sweat from his brow with the back of his hand and grinned at her. "So did I."

She laughed in spite of herself. "You are incorrigible."

"I certainly hope so."

The next fifteen or twenty minutes were spent clearing the entrance to the cave. Finally there was an opening large enough for a man to comfortably pass through.

Strong held up the lantern they had brought along with them and peered into the shadowy passageway. "I'm going to go ahead and test a few of the supports, take a look around, see what it's like inside. I want you to stay put until I come back for you. Do you understand?"

Kit understood. She just didn't like being left behind. She knew it would sound like a cliché, but she said it anyway. "Please be careful."

"Trust me, I will be."

"Don't be gone long."

"Not any longer than is absolutely necessary."

She was having second thoughts already. "Are you sure this is a good idea?"

Strong paused, leaned over, brought his mouth down on hers in a kiss that left her breathless, and disappeared into the black cavern.

She paced back and forth in front of the mine entrance.

She checked her watch every thirty seconds.

She said a prayer, then another.

She chewed off her fingernails.

She stopped and peered into the cave as far as she could see—which wasn't far.

She cursed the fates, Strong O'Kelly, Michael O'Kelly, Peg Rhodes, Cactus Moser and, in general, most of the male sex.

Five minutes passed.

Then ten.

Kit decided that the fool—had it been the renowned poet John Milton himself?—who'd said, "They also serve who only stand and wait," hadn't done much standing or waiting. She was in agony.

In fact, she was about to say to hell with Strong's instructions for her to stay put, when she saw the yellow glow of the lantern, and he emerged.

She didn't utter a word. She just went to him and wrapped her arms tightly around his waist. She hung on to him for dear life. She buried her face in the front of his shirt. She shed a tear or two and heaved an enormous sigh of relief.

He was hot and sweaty, she didn't give a damn. His shirt was dirty, she could have cared less. He was covered from head to toe with a fine layer of dust, which now streaked her face, her sweater, her jeans—she welcomed it.

"Obviously I should venture into the unknown more often," joked Strong as he tipped her head back and gazed down into her face. "That was a heck of a welcome home, lady."

"I was worried about you," she admitted.

"I'm fine."

"You were gone so long."

"Ten minutes to be exact."

"It seemed like a lot longer out here," she informed him.

"Actually, it seemed like a lot shorter than ten minutes in there," he said. "Are you okay?"

She nodded. "I am now."

Strong's tanned face suddenly dissolved into a broad smile. "We've found The Lucky Cuss."

"Are you sure?"

He was excited. "Almost sure. Pretty sure. Ninety-nine percent sure."

Now she was getting excited, too. "Is it safe to go in?"

He gave a decisive nod of his head. "Once you're past the entrance, you are essentially in a cavern. I could stand up without any problem. The place is solid rock, and rock solid. Believe me, it would take a *major* earthquake to bring it down on our heads."

"And the gold?" she asked eagerly. "Is there any gold?"

Strong's expression was inscrutable. "Come see for yourself," was all he would say.

He went first, taking her by the hand, guiding her through the narrow entrance, then into the main room of the cavern.

"It's huge in here!" Kit exclaimed, and heard her voice echo off the walls.

Strong held up the lantern, but it only had enough power to partially illuminate the vast darkness. "I would estimate this place to be thirty feet at the highest point and somewhere between forty and fifty feet across."

"That is huge." Kit gripped Strong's hand until she knew her knuckles were white. "Did I see something sparkle on the wall over there?"

"Let's go take a look," he casually suggested.

They made their way to the opposite side of the cavern, and Strong held up the lantern.

"Dear God—" Kit could scarcely breathe.

There were veins of bright yellow—some as thick as a man's thumb, some even wider—running through the solid rock wall. It was everywhere. Deposits of bright shiny metal embedded in rock of every size, shape and color.

Gold.

Kit could feel the color mount to her cheeks. "There must be a fortune here. A king's ransom. Millions of dollars. Maybe more."

"Maybe."

Gold.

"Strong, you're rich."

"Do you think so?" he asked in an odd voice.

"Of course. The mine was your grandfather's, and now it's yours."

Gold.

"And if I weren't rich?"

Kit turned and studied his profile in the lantern light. "What do you mean?"

He looked at her. "Would it matter to you?"

"If you were rich or poor?"

"That's the question."

She realized he wasn't joking. He was serious. Deadly serious. "It didn't matter to me ten years ago. It matters even less to me now."

"I wish I could believe that." His voice dwindled away.

"I can prove it."

"How?"

"We turn our backs on this place and we walk out of here right now."

"Just like that?"

"Just like that."

"Leave all of this behind?"

"Leave it all behind. Never come back. Never speak of it again. Dynamite it. Bury it. Cover it up with brush. I don't care. I don't want it. I never have." Kit meant every word. "Money has never been important to me." She shrugged. "Perhaps because I've always had money."

"What is important to you, then?"

"You are," she declared with a vehemence that surprised both of them. "You are important to me."

Strong took a step toward her. "Let me show you something, darling."

"Now ain't that just about the prettiest durn thing you ever did see," came a familiar androgynous voice from behind them.

They both turned.

There was a dark figure standing at the entrance to the cave, a shadowy, indistinguishable object held in one hand, a flashlight in the other, its bright beam focused on the two of them.

The new arrival was dressed in faded overalls and a plaid shirt with the elbows worn through. There was a pair of old work boots on the feet, and a billed cap was pulled down over the eyes and a good portion of the face.

"Makes it a whole lot easier you two not wantin' the gold. Yup, sure does make it easier on t'all of us."

"I recognize that voice," Kit whispered under her breath to Strong.

"Shush now, girl. No need for you to be talkin'."

Kit felt the man beside her reach for her hand and give it a reassuring squeeze.

"Who are 'all of us'?" Strong inquired nonchalantly.

"Don't try to get smart with me, young man," said the husky voice. "I know you to be a fast-talkin' lawyer. Never did trust lawyers."

"Which one are you? At least tell us that much," Strong urged in a quiet, determined voice.

"Which one?"

"Which one of Michael O'Kelly's former partners? Are you Peg Rhodes or Cactus Moser?"

That brought a delighted cackle from the oldster. "I had you both fooled the whole time. You never knowed. You never even guessed."

All of a sudden an idea occurred to Kit. Something she should have thought of before. Something she should have thought of a long time ago.

She let go of Strong's hand and took one step toward the beam of light. "You're not either one, are you?" she said in a soft voice.

"Stay where you are, girl."

She took another step closer to the flashlight. "You're not Peg Rhodes or Cactus Moser."

"Don't come no closer." There was a slight quiver in the elderly voice. "I got me a gun."

Kit took a deep breath. "You won't shoot me."

"What makes you say that?"

"I don't think you've ever hurt anybody in your whole life. I don't think you mean to start now."

"You got no way of knowin' that," cried out the stranger.

"What you did, you did out of love. Wasn't that right?"

"You're confusin' me, girl."

Kit's confidence in her own judgment was growing by the moment. "Why don't you put the gun down before someone gets hurt by accident? That way we can talk woman to woman."

"Woman to woman?" Strong repeated in an incredulous tone.

"How'd you know?" the bent figure asked Kit.

"Maybe some sixth sense told me. Maybe it was feminine intuition. Maybe it was because I understand what it is to love a man with all of your heart and soul."

There was a soft cry. "Lordy, lordy."

"Why not put the gun down?"

"Don't have no bullets in it, anyway," confessed the dejected figure at the cave entrance.

Strong and Kit came closer. They could clearly see the old woman now.

"Are you Cactus Moser's girlfriend?" asked Kit.

The head nodded.

She quietly inquired, "What's your name?"

The head came up. The cap was pushed back to reveal sad eyes filled with tears. "My name is Ida Pearl. Ida Pearl Go-on."

Fifteen

―

"**Y**ou want to tell us about it now, Ida Pearl?" urged Strong, once the three of them were out in the daylight again and perched on rocks at the cave entrance.

The old woman looked over at him and blew her nose in the tissue kindly provided by Kit. "Now I see you in the light, you sure do look like that rascal Michael O'Kelly. Specially through the eyes. You got his eyes. You know that, don't you?"

"Yes, I know I got Pap's eyes," he said, unsmiling.

"'Course you're a much bigger man."

"So they tell me."

"Heard you went on to make somethin' of yourself." She gave him a watery smile.

"I'm a lawyer. But you already know that, remember?"

"There's lawyers and then there's lawyers."

"That's true."

Kit interjected, "Strong is a wonderful attorney who does the best he can to help everyone."

Ida Pearl gave a decisive nod of her head. "Done the O'Kelly name proud, then, boy."

"Man," he corrected.

Her old eyes were still shrewd. "I can see that. You sure is a man."

"I am a man."

"Rumor has it, you been redoin' the Stone House, makin' it good an' solid again."

"I've been working on it."

"Made it harder for me to do what I had to do," she confessed to him.

"Did it?"

"I figured whatever Michael O'Kelly had left behind would be in that durn house. Then I gets there and finds you moved in." She shook her head. "I never done wrong before like trespassin'. Leastwise not unless I was huntin' for rabbits or the like. I do apologize for sneaking into your garage and for stealing the picture of you and the girl here."

His green eyes narrowed to slits. "I didn't like that."

She heaved a sigh and shook her head from side to side. "I didn't figure you would."

"You had no right."

"I know." Ida Pearl completely agreed with him.

"If you were a man, I'd take you out behind the shed and teach you a lesson or two you wouldn't forget."

"Guess I'm lucky I'm not a man."

"I could still get you thrown in jail for doing a damn fool thing like that."

"You're plenty mad at Ida Pearl, ain't you?" she surmised, wiping at her weathered face and stuffing the used tissue in her shirt pocket.

"I can't deny that I'm mad at you, Ida Pearl," Strong told her truthfully. "I want to know why. I want to know why you did it."

She pulled off her billed hat, ran her gnarled, arthritic fingers through her white hair and declared stubbornly, "I had my reasons."

"Was it for the gold?"

That brought her head up. Tears sprang to her eyes and ran down her wrinkled cheeks, but she paid them no mind. "For the gold?"

"Did you do it for the gold?" Strong repeated, driving home his point.

"You think I did it for that dang-blasted gold? I hate the stuff. It ruined my life. It ruined *his* life. It's a sickness. It's an addiction. It's worse than booze, or broads, or any horrible drug you can dump into a body." Ida Pearl stopped and gathered her thoughts. When she went on, there was a lifetime of sadness in the husky voice. "You know what they say about gold. They say it's a fever. That once it gets into a man's blood the only cure is death."

Kit reached out and gently placed her hand on the other woman's arm. "Who did you do it for?"

Ida Pearl Go-on lifted her aging chin and stared off toward the mountains on the horizon. "I done it for him."

"Him?"

"And I done it for myself."

"Yourself?"

"I wanted to give him his last wish. I wanted to see his eyes when he held it in his hands, when he touched it, when he knew it was his. Then he could die happy."

"Where is Peg Rhodes?"

"That old reprobate," she said, snorting. "Peg moved out to Californ-i-a to live with his niece after he lost his leg in that mining accident."

Strong looked over at Kit. They were both surprised by that news.

"You didn't know about ol' Peg, did you?"

Strong answered for both of them. "No, we didn't."

She was chatty on the subject. "All that sunshine seems to agree with him. Least that's what he wrote on a picture postcard he sent us once."

"When was that?" asked Kit.

Ida Pearl contemplated her answer for half a minute, maybe longer. "Must have been back in '79. Yup, t'were the summer of 1979."

Strong still wanted answers. He wanted it done once and for all. "And Cactus Moser?"

She didn't say anything for the longest time, then stated simply, "Cactus ain't goin' to make it."

Strong leaned forward and rested his forearms on his thighs. "What do you mean, Cactus isn't going to make it?"

Her mouth quivered slightly. She sunk her teeth into her bottom lip. It was a while before she replied. "The Big C's got him."

"The Big C?"

"The cancer's got him."

Strong watched as Kit dealt gently with the old woman. "Is he very sick?"

Ida Pearl Go-on nodded her head. "He's real sick. He don't have much longer."

"Then you did it for Cactus."

Embarrassed, the elderly woman looked away. "I wanted to give him the one thing he wanted most in his whole damn life—that blasted gold."

"How did you find out about it?" asked Strong.

She was more than willing to tell him, both of them. "The cancer drugs sometimes made Cactus kind of crazy in his head. He would go on and on about all kinds of things. He told me again and again about the partnership him and Clester Rhodes and Michael O'Kelly signed back in '38. He talked lots about The Lucky Cuss. How it was going to make them all rich. How they was going to live like kings. How they was going to eat off gold plates and drink out of gold cups and sleep in gold beds like that place the king had in France."

"Versailles?"

"Yup, that's the place." She rubbed her eyes. "I knew it was all a crazy dream. But it was Cactus's dream."

"And you love him so much, don't you?" said Kit.

"I do. Don't know why... all he ever loved was the gold," Ida Pearl confessed. "Anyways, once the doctors told me there weren't no hope, I begun to hatch my plans. Cactus loved to talk about the old days. It weren't difficult to get it out of him. I been working on it for near six months now."

"You've been very clever," said Strong, stretching out his legs in front of him.

"I can be when I got to be," was all she said.

"You went to a great deal of trouble to find out about our annulment papers," he prompted.

"I knew this lawyer who weren't quite as honest as the day is long. He done some digging around for me. We was both surprised by what we found. We figured you would be, too." She looked from one to the other. "You didn't know you was still married, did you?"

Strong's jaw was steel. "No. We didn't."

"We was sorry, Cactus and me, that the past had to be dredged up like that. We didn't mean you or the girl no harm, Strong. We only did what we had to do so Cactus could have his gold."

"You frightened me the night you called," Kit told the woman truthfully.

"I know, girl. I know. I'll go to my grave feelin' real bad about that."

"The threats you sent us were unkind," added Kit.

"They were. I'm sure the Good Lord is going to punish me for every one of the sins I done committed," Ida Pearl said, and quickly crossed herself. "I do expect I'll be in purgatory for quite a spell."

Strong looked at the old woman, her aging face drawn into deeper and deeper lines of worry and regret. What she had done made sense in an awful, wasteful, tragic way. If she had been young, if she had been a man, he would have taken great delight in beating the living tar out of her. But she was just an old lady—just a lonely, old lady.

"Whatcha gonna do now?" inquired Ida Pearl. "You gonna haul me off to jail? Or can I go back to Jasper long enough to say goodbye to Cactus?"

Strong drew a weary hand across his brow and thought for a minute or two. Then he made his decision. He knew it was the right thing to do. "Neither one."

She couldn't comprehend what he was telling her, that was apparent. "Neither one?"

"You're not going to jail. You don't have to say goodbye to Cactus, at least not for a while."

"I don't understand. I don't understand," the old woman repeated in her confusion.

Strong stood up, stretched his aching back, and beckoned to both Kit and Ida Pearl. "I have something to show the two of you."

"Something to show us?" Even Kit was taken aback.

"Follow me," he commanded and, turning, went back inside The Lucky Cuss.

"What is it?" asked Kit.

Strong took them to the wall of rock and held up the lantern. "It's beautiful, isn't it?"

"Yes."

"Shore is."

"Looks like gold, doesn't it?"

"What do you mean, it *looks* like gold?" challenged Kit.

"Ain't it gold?"

Strong took his knife and pried off a nugget the size of his thumb. He held it up to the light. "Pyrite, the most common and widely distributed sulfide mineral. It's a compound of iron and sulfur. The name comes from the Greek word for fire. If we strike it with a piece of metal—" he set the nugget to one side, then brought the machete blade forcefully down on the stone "—it creates a spark."

"Well, I'll be—" exclaimed Ida Pearl Go-on.

Strong told them more. "Sometimes it's called iron pyrite. Sometimes, because prospectors were misled by its bright metallic luster and golden yellow color, it's often been called fool's gold."

Kit's voice was hushed. "Fool's gold."

Ida Pearl slapped her corduroy pantleg and crowed in an incredulous voice, "That's it, ain't it? That's the reason Michael O'Kelly went to his grave without sharin' his fortune."

Strong spelled it out loud and clear. "There never was any fortune."

"And there never was any gold?"

"There never was any gold. Pap knew it all along. The Lucky Cuss was *and* is worthless."

After a minute Kit asked him, "How do you know your grandfather realized it was a worthless mine?"

"Remember the sign behind him in the photograph?"

"Yes."

"It was half-obscured and too small for us to read even with the telephoto lens, wasn't it?"

"It was."

Strong leaned over and picked up a half-rotted board from the floor of the cave. "I found this when I first came into the mine."

Ida Pearl squinted at the writing. "Can't see it proper in this light."

Kit scanned the carved words, but insisted, "Read it to us, Strong."

He held up the half-century-old board and read the words out loud, "'All that glitters is not gold. Signed, yours truly, Michael O'Kelly, miner and gentleman.'"

Sixteen

——

"**I**'ll tell you what I'm going to do, Ida Pearl," said Strong once they were outside The Lucky Cuss. "I will forget this whole thing ever happened under two conditions...."

The old woman's mouth dropped down to her second chin. "You mean you're willin' to forgive and forget?"

"Under two conditions," he reiterated.

She put her stooped shoulders back as far as they would go. She was prepared to take her punishment. "What're the two conditions?"

He stood before the aging woman, his shoulders broad and strong; his hair dark and windswept; his face handsome, intelligent, honest; his eyes vivid green, emerald green—Irish green. They flashed in the late afternoon sun.

Kit didn't think she had ever seen Strong look more beautiful than he did at that moment.

"First," he said with a solemnity that befit the occasion and the circumstance, "you will give me your word you will never ever do anything like this again."

"I give you my solemn word," vowed Ida Pearl, "so help me God."

"You swear it."

"I swear it."

Strong took something from the pocket of his shirt, reached for her weathered, wrinkled hand, opened the palm and dropped an object into it.

"Why, mercy sakes!" exclaimed Ida Pearl Go-on with disbelief. "It's the large gold nugget."

"Not quite *gold*," Strong reminded her. "But maybe Cactus won't know the difference."

She understood immediately. The tears formed on the tips of her snow-white eyelashes. "Cactus won't know. His eyes ain't what they used to be."

"That is my second condition."

The woman frowned. "What is?"

"I want you to take the 'gold nugget' to Cactus. You make him promise to keep it a secret, and then you tell him wondrous stories about The Lucky Cuss. You keep his dream alive as long as he lives." Strong looked past both Ida Pearl and Kit to the mountains on the horizon. "Every man has to have his dream. Every woman, too."

"You're a fine man, Strong O'Kelly," declared Ida Pearl. "I don't believe I ever met one finer."

Kit fought back the tears.

The woman turned and squinted at her. "You got a good man there, girl."

"I know," she managed.

"You take care of him. Don't you be foolish like I was. If you love him then tell him so."

"You'd better head for home now," prompted Strong. "It's getting late, and Cactus will be wondering where you are."

"I—I don't know how to t-thank you," the woman stammered.

"You don't have to thank me. You only have to remember our two conditions."

"I'll remember."

Then Ida Pearl Go-on safely stowed the iron pyrite nugget in her pants' pocket, gave a nod to Kit and held out her hand to Strong O'Kelly.

He shook it, being the gentleman he was.

"I think it's time we headed back, too," he remarked to Kit once Ida Pearl was on her way. He put his head back and gazed up at the sky. "It'll be dark in another hour."

With her usual efficiency Kit began to gather up the supplies and equipment they had brought with them. "Then we'd better get a move on. I like to be home before dark," she informed him.

For some reason that brought a smile to Strong O'Kelly's lips.

They were in the Jeep and bumping along over the hill and grassy meadow, heading back toward the dirt road and civilization before either of them spoke.

"I've been thinking," Strong started out.

"About what?"

"In a funny kind of way, Ida Pearl and Cactus Moser did us a favor."

"Did us a favor? How do you figure that?"

Strong rubbed his jaw thoughtfully. "Well, the way I see it, without their interference we could have gone on forever not knowing we were still married to each other."

"That's true," she conceded.

But was that good or bad? That was the question Kit was afraid to ask both Strong and herself.

"Canned ravioli," grumbled Strong as he pulled into the driveway of the Stone House an hour later.

Kit looked at him askance. "What about canned ravioli?"

"I think it's all I have on hand for dinner."

She bit the inside of her mouth, and managed not to smile. "Is the cupboard bare?"

He shifted the vehicle into park. "I don't stock a lot of food supplies. I'm not much of a cook."

"What do you usually eat?" she asked with a pang.

He shrugged. "Pizza. Fast food. Microwave stuff. Whatever is quick and easy." Green eyes engaged hers. "Do you want to get cleaned up and go out somewhere for dinner?"

She glanced down at her dusty jeans and sweater, her dusty hiking boots, her dusty jacket. She was more tired than hungry. "Nah—we'll make do. I think I spotted another pepperoni pizza in the back of your freezer."

Strong seemed relieved. "Let's leave the mining equipment in the Jeep," he suggested. "I'll unpack it in the morning."

That was fine with her. All Kit wanted to do was take a hot shower and change into clean clothes.

Several hours later they were both showered, fed—if not well-fed—and sitting on the sofa in the living room. There was a definite chill in the air; there often was in the evening in the mountains. Strong lit the kindling and logs already laid in the fireplace, and soon had a blazing fire going. The only other light in the room came from a small lamp on a table in the corner. It was the perfect romantic setting.

For all the good it did her.

Kit carefully folded her hands on her lap, then unfolded them. She rearranged the tapestry pillows behind her for the third time in as many minutes. She fussed. She fidgeted. She cleared her throat and opened her mouth to speak, then shut it again without saying a word.

Why was she so uncomfortable? Why was she so nervous? She felt like a schoolgirl about to go on her first date. For crying out loud, the man was her husband!

That was the problem, of course.

The next few minutes, certainly the next hour or two, might well determine her entire future.

Strong fiddled with the logs for several more minutes, wiped his palms on the legs of his blue jeans and awkwardly sat down beside her again.

She heard him draw in a long breath and let it out slowly. "I think it's time we talked."

Kit watched the fire lick and leap around the dry logs. The flames were burning brightly; their color changing from blue to red to yellow. "I think it's time, too."

"Where do you want to begin?"

It only seemed logical to suggest, "At the beginning."

"The beginning?"

She plucked at a loose thread on her sweater. "I think the first thing we need to talk about is what happened ten years ago."

"I agree."

Kit swallowed with extreme difficulty. She didn't want to, but she had to say it. "You lied to me."

Strong immediately countered with an accusation of his own. "You didn't stand by me."

After a lengthy pause she said, "We're right back where we started from. Nothing has changed."

"Plenty of things have changed," he claimed.

"*Some* things have changed," she tempered.

A tense frown bracketed his stern lips. He drove his hands through his hair and swore under his breath. "I was so damn crazy about you."

Suddenly Kit wanted to weep. She sunk her teeth into her bottom lip. "I was crazy about you, too."

In a rapid, deep, unnatural voice, he said, "I almost didn't make it after we broke up."

"Me, either," she finally admitted, twisting the strand of loose thread around her finger.

For the first time Strong seemed to be on the edge of losing his composure. "I loved you and I hated you."

She directed a frenzied whisper toward him. "I was so hurt. It took me a long time to get over it."

"It took me a long time, as well."

She couldn't let it go. She had to know. "Why?"

"Why what?"

"Why did you lie to me?"

His jaw muscles were jumping. "You mean about my age?"

The thread around her finger snapped in two. "Yes, about your age."

Strong blew out his breath. "I guess I was afraid if you knew I was only seventeen you wouldn't go out with me."

"I wouldn't have," said Kit with simplicity.

"So I was right."

"You were right and you were wrong. You shouldn't have lied to me," she insisted.

Strong reached out and placed his hands on her shoulders and firmly turned her toward him. "I wanted you so badly I would have done anything. *Anything*, Kit. Do you understand? Adding a few years to my age didn't seem like a big deal."

"It was to me." Years of frustration surfaced. "You were a boy, Strong. I married a boy."

Like a match touched to dynamite, he exploded. "I was never a boy, damn it. When we were married I was a man."

"You were seventeen!" she cried out.

"So what?" he challenged, his voice rising, rich with anger. "I knew a hell of a lot more about life than you did. *You* were the innocent one, Kit. *You* were the naive one. *You* were the inexperienced one. Or have you forgotten?"

She hadn't forgotten. It was true. All true.

She pushed a little further. "Why didn't you tell me the truth after we were married?"

Strong hesitated. "I intended to. But before I had the chance, your father did it for me."

Kit waited for the pain to increase to anguish. "I wish you had told me."

"I wish you had stood by me."

"I couldn't."

He speared her with a long stare. "Why not? We loved each other. We were married. Why did you let me walk away without a fight? Hell, without a single damn word?"

"I was so embarrassed."

"Embarrassed?" The word shot out of his mouth.

"Yes, embarrassed. I was embarrassed and mortified to find myself sleeping with, crazy in love with— married to—a seventeen-year-old."

There! It was all finally out in the open. She'd admitted at last what had been bothering her since the day they'd returned from their honeymoon at the Stone House.

Strong shook his head from side to side and muttered grimly, "You were really hung up on the numbers, weren't you?"

"Yes," she said, wearily admitting defeat.

"Are you now?"

She was befuddled.

He expounded. "What do the numbers mean now, Kit? The difference between our ages hasn't changed. It's exactly the same. Five years."

She wasn't certain what Strong was driving at, but her heart was slamming against her chest. "But you're twenty-seven and I'm thirty-two. We're both consenting adults."

"That's right. It's no longer a factor."

He leaned toward her and all she saw for a moment were his eyes. His vivid green eyes, his Irish green eyes, his emerald green eyes. "So what happens now?"

She swallowed. "We forgive each other, even if we can't forget."

"A good idea."

"We acknowledge that we both were young, that we both made mistakes, that we were both at fault."

"I was young. I made mistakes. I was wrong," stated Strong.

"Ditto," came out in a husky voice.

He looked intently into her eyes. "I forgive you and I forgive myself."

"I forgive you and I forgive myself," Kit echoed.

Strong got up and nervously paced the floor of the living room. Then he went down on his haunches, added another log to the fire and stared into the flames.

"I can understand Pap and Peg Rhodes and old Cactus Moser," he told her. "I can understand every man who has ever caught the fever."

"The fever?"

"The gold fever," he answered, without turning.

"I—I don't get it," she stammered. "I thought you weren't interested in gold."

He shot her a look. "I'm not. But *you* are a fever. *You* are an addiction. *You* are in my blood and death will be the only cure."

It was suddenly very quiet. The only sound was the crackling of the fire.

Kit dared not move. "Why do you want to be cured?"

His reply was low and fervent. "I can't spend my life wanting a woman I can't have."

She took a deep breath and blurted out, "Why can't you have her?"

That stopped him cold. Strong slowly rose to his feet and stared down at her. "What are you saying, Kit?"

Her hands gestured restlessly. "I—I thought you knew. I thought you understood."

He took two steps toward her. "Well, I don't and I didn't. You explain it to me."

"It was when we were in The Lucky Cuss. I was speaking to Ida Pearl, but I meant the words for you, too."

Dear God, he hadn't understood. She had thought he simply didn't care, not in that way, not anymore.

"Say them again," Strong prompted. "Say the words again."

"I told Ida Pearl that I understood the reason why she'd done it for Cactus. I told her that I understood what it was like to love a man with all of your heart and soul."

"Why is that?"

Kit braced herself. "Because I love you with all of my heart and soul."

He took another step toward her. "Not *loved*...past tense? *Love*...present tense?"

Kit gazed at Strong and knew it was there in her eyes for him to see—the truth, and nothing but the truth—all he had to do was believe.

Her voice was low, but weighed with conviction. "I love you, Strong O'Kelly. I fell in love with you the first day we met and I have been in love with you every day since."

He still held back. "And last night? What was last night? We said there were no promises, no past, no future, no yesterday, no tomorrow. There was only the moment."

"Last night—" she struggled to stay calm and halfway composed "—was last night. It was sex."

He flinched.

She continued. "It was lust. It was passion. It was physical and mental and emotional. It was crazy. It was wild and wonderful. But most of all, it was loving."

Strong dropped down beside her on the sofa. "Are you certain?"

"I'm certain." She had never been more so. "I made love with you, Strong. I love you."

Now it was his turn to say the words.

Instead, he laughed and swore under his breath, "I'll be a sonofa—"

"What about you?" she burst out, catching him by surprise.

He frowned. "What about me?"

"How do you feel? What was last night to you? Tell me. I want to know. I want to hear the words."

His eyes were smoldering dark green, like rare emeralds just taken from the earth. "I have told you how I feel. I told you last night."

"Say the words again."

Strong recited them like a love poem. "When you cry, I cry. When you laugh, I laugh. When you're afraid, then I'm afraid for you. When you hurt, I feel the pain. When one day you die, that is the day I die, too." Holding her chin in his hand, he gazed into her eyes and declared, "I love you, Kit."

"Thank God!" she said, half prayer, half incantation, as she kissed him.

Then Strong swept her into his arms and laid her down on the rug in front of the fire. He stretched out alongside her. "A long time ago I told you I wanted to make love to you in a real bed, on a white sandy beach, in a meadow of summer wildflowers, in front of a winter's fire."

"I remember," she murmured, reaching up to caress his face, to trace the outline of his mouth with her fingertips.

"I promised myself I would make love to you day and night. I would make love to you forever."

Kit's hands went to the buttons of his shirt. She smiled meaningfully. "I think this is as good a time as any to start, don't you?"

"There's no time like the present," he agreed as they began to undress each other with a light and loving touch.

But when she reached for the buckle at his waist, Strong became impatient. He rolled away from her long enough to remove the rest of his clothing. Then he stood there in the firelight in his natural glory, gazing down at her with eyes that spoke of love and passion.

God, he was still the most beautiful human being she had ever seen.

"Promises. Promises," she muttered.

"What did you say?"

She repeated louder. "Promises. Promises."

Strong got that certain look in his eyes that she knew all too well. "That's right." He snapped his fingers together as if he had just remembered something. "This morning I said I would show you how I deal with a sassy wife."

"Actually," she pointed out, "you said first you would *tell* me how you deal with a sassy wife."

He came down beside her and slowly—excruciatingly so—stripped the remainder of her clothing from her body. "Maybe we'll show *and* tell," he gritted through his teeth as his hands began to move over her.

He caressed her from the nape of her neck to the vulnerable spot behind her ear, along the delicate bones at the base of her throat and over her bare shoulders. His mouth followed where his hands had been only moments before. He seemed to deliberately avoid those most erotic places, tantalizing her, teasing her, torturing her.

"Strong—" she cried out in frustration.

"What is it, my love?"

"Please!"

"Please what?"

"Please make love to me."

He grinned at her. It was a totally masculine grin. It was a completely self-satisfied grin. It was a slightly wicked grin. "Well, let me see. I wonder if I'm up for it."

She gazed down at his manhood wedged between their passion-slick bodies and began to laugh. She couldn't help it. He was huge and hard as a rock.

She lifted her face to his and declared, "Oh, I think you're up to it."

"Perhaps we'd better make sure," he growled erotically as he brought his mouth down on hers.

Strong kissed her until she didn't have a solitary thought left in her head. His tongue flicked back and forth over her lips and delved deeply into her throat. His kisses were gentle and tender, then fierce and demanding. It was a wild roller coaster ride. It was fireworks on the Fourth of July. It was the sun beating down on the desert and the lightning during a thunderstorm.

Then he moved lower and began to suckle on her breasts until she was mad, quite mad. She instinctively arched her back. She separated her thighs. She clawed at his flesh with her fingernails.

She was wild with the need he had created in her, and she expressed that need with her own hands, her own mouth, her own tongue.

"Dear God, Kit," he cried out as her lips sought that most intimate knowledge of him.

He was a creature of contrasts. He was hard and smooth. He was hot and heavy. He was fine and graceful. He was masculine and blunt.

She loved the feel of him, the smell of him, the taste of him. This was the man she loved. This was her husband. There were no barriers between them. There were no taboos.

By the time Strong slipped his fingers into her, she was all warm and wet and willing, ready to receive him, begging to receive him. She wanted him now more than she had ever wanted him before. There was a depth, a commitment, a lasting promise in each touch, each caress.

Kneeling above her for a moment, Strong straddled her body. He was as aroused as Kit could ever remember in all the times she had seen him in a state of sexual excitement. She took him in her hands, held him between her palms, brought him right up to the velvet soft opening of her body.

There was a fine sheen of perspiration on Strong's forehead and face. His body was damp, taut. His hair was straight and a single strand fell forward onto his face. The muscles of his chest and arms quivered with the strain of holding back.

"I know what the real pot of gold is at the end of the rainbow," he managed to utter, holding on to his self-control, his very sanity, it seemed, by sheer willpower alone.

"What is it?" asked Kit as she moved against him, pulled him into her, her muscles contracting around him, drawing him deeper, ever deeper.

"Love," he declared, and surged into her body. He thrust again and again, faster and faster, filling her to the hilt.

Kit wrapped her legs around him, and they began to move toward that shattering moment of climax. She arched into the increasing rhythm of his movements.

As Strong drove into her with his *last* breath, with his body's final burst of energy, he shouted again, "Love!"

Epilogue

The second wedding of Katherine St. Clair and Strongarm Carlos Michael O'Kelly took place on a perfect afternoon in the middle of June. The sky was blue. The sun was a bright canary yellow. The temperature was temperate.

The ceremony was held in a beautiful old Spanish chapel, discreetly decorated with an Irish shamrock and the Navajo symbol for peace and harmony.

In front of God, their families and their friends, Kit and Strong repeated the vows they had first spoken to each other ten years before.

"I take this woman..."

"I take this man..."

"...To love, honor and cherish..."

" . . . For richer, for poorer . . ."

" . . . In sickness and in health, as long as we both shall live."

There was not a dry eye in the chapel. Even Sally Bradford, the newly appointed manager of the Phoenix branch of St. Clair Enterprises, and Mildred Leeper were dabbing at their cheeks with damp tissues.

The ceremony concluded with words the couple had written themselves.

In a strong, clear voice that could be heard in every corner of the church, Kit declared, "Strong, you are my past, my present, my future. You are more to me than riches and treasures." Her voice softened. "You are my one and only love."

Then she presented her husband with her prize possession—the antique Navajo necklace created long ago by Slender Maker of Silver.

Strong placed a "gold" eternity bracelet around his wife's wrist—the metal had come from his grandfather's mine, as the two of them well knew—and vowed, "Kit, you are my past, my present, my future. You are more to me than riches and treasures." His deep baritone broke for an instant. "You are more to me than life itself."

The minister continued, "By the authority vested in me as a Minister of the Church, I declare that Strong and Katherine are husband and wife, according to the Ordinance of God, and the law of the State of Arizona. Whom therefore God hath joined together, let no man put asunder."

There was no mistaking the look of satisfaction on the handsome face of Strongarm O'Kelly.

The minister added with a smile, "You may now kiss your wife."

Strong leaned over and, in the instant before he kissed her, whispered lovingly against Kit's lips, "I always was a lucky cuss, darling."

* * * * *

What a year for romance!

Silhouette has five fabulous romance collections coming your way in 1993. Written by popular Silhouette authors, each story is a sensuous tale of love and life—as only Silhouette can give you!

Three bachelors are footloose and fancy-free... until now.
(March)

Heartwarming stories that celebrate the joy of motherhood.
(May)

Put some sizzle into your summer reading with three of Silhouette's hottest authors.
(June)

Take a walk on the dark side of love— with tales just perfect for those misty autumn nights.
(October)

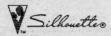

Share in the joy of yuletide romance with four award-winning Silhouette authors.
(November)

A romance for all seasons—it's always time for romance with Silhouette!

Silhouette
CHRISTMAS
Stories
1992

Experience the beauty of Yuletide romance with Silhouette Christmas Stories 1992—a collection of heartwarming stories by favorite Silhouette authors.

JONI'S MAGIC by Mary Lynn Baxter
HEARTS OF HOPE by Sondra Stanford
THE NIGHT SANTA CLAUS RETURNED by Marie Ferrarrella
BASKET OF LOVE by Jeanne Stephens

Also available this year are three popular early editions of Silhouette Christmas Stories—1986, 1987 and 1988. Look for these and you'll be well on your way to a complete collection of the best in holiday romance.

Plus, as an added bonus, you can receive a FREE keepsake Christmas ornament. Just collect four proofs of purchase from any November or December 1992 Harlequin or Silhouette series novels, or from any Harlequin or Silhouette Christmas collection, and receive a beautiful dated brass Christmas candle ornament.

Mail this certificate along with four (4) proof-of-purchase coupons, plus $1.50 postage and handling (check or money order—do not send cash), payable to Silhouette Books, to: **In the U.S.:** P.O. Box 9057, Buffalo, NY 14269-9057; **In Canada:** P.O. Box 622, Fort Erie, Ontario, L2A 5X3.

ONE PROOF OF PURCHASE	Name: _____
	_____
	Address: _____
	_____
	City: _____
	State/Province: _____
SX92POP	Zip/Postal Code: _____

093 KAG